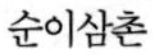

순이삼촌

아시아에서는 《바이링궐 에디션 한국 대표 소설》을 기획하여 한국의 우수한 문학을 주제별로 엄선해 국내외 독자들에게 소개합니다. 이 기획은 국내외 우수한 번역가들이 참여하여 원작의 품격을 최대한 살렸습니다. 문학을 통해 아시아의 정체성과 가치를 살피는 데 주력해 온 아시아는 한국인의 삶을 넓고 깊게 이해하는 데 이 기획이 기여하기를 기대합니다.

Asia Publishers presents some of the very best modern Korean literature to readers worldwide through its new Korean literature series 〈Bi-lingual Edition Modern Korean Literature〉. We are proud and happy to offer it in the most authoritative translation by renowned translators of Korean literature. We hope that this series helps to build solid bridges between citizens of the world and Koreans through a rich in-depth understanding of Korea.

바이링궐 에디션 한국 대표 소설 003
Bi-lingual Edition Modern Korean Literature 003

Sun-i Samch'on

현기영

순이삼촌

Hyun Ki-young

ASIA
PUBLISHERS

Contents

순이삼촌

Sun-i Samch'on

내가 그 얻기 어려운 이틀간의 휴가를 간신히 따내가지고 고향을 찾아간 것은 음력 섣달 열여드레인 할아버지 제삿날에 때를 맞춘 것이었다. 할머니 탈상 때 내려가 보고 지금까지이니 그동안 팔 년이란 세월이 흐른 것이었다. 바쁜 직장 핑계 대고 조부모 제사에 한 번도 다녀오지 못했으니 큰아버지나 사촌 길수 형은 편지 글발에 내색하지는 않았지만 속으로 무던히도 욕을 하고 있을 터였다. 물론 일본에 있는 아버지가 제사 때가 되면 잊지 않고 제숫감 마련에 쓰고도 남아 얼마간 가용에 보탬이 될 만큼 넉넉하게 큰집으로 송금하는 모양이지만, 그렇다고 내가 선산을 못 돌아보고 기제사에 참례 못 하는 죄스러움이

It was December 18 by the lunar calendar, the memorial day for my grandfather, when I visited my hometown on a precious two-day vacation I was lucky to get. It had been eight years since my previous trip, for the second memorial day for my grandmother. Since I had missed all the subsequent memorial services for my grandparents with the lame excuse of a busy work schedule, my uncle and my cousin Kil-su probably didn't have many good things to say about me even if they didn't exactly reveal their thoughts in the letter. I am quite certain that my father in Japan remembered every year without fail to send them generous sums of money

가벼워지는 것은 아니었다. 그러다가 요 며칠 전에 큰아버지의 부름을 받고 만 것이었다. 가족 묘지 매입 문제로 상의할 일이 있으니 할아버지 제사일에 맞춰 내려오라는 편지 내용이었다. 편지투로 보아 이번엔 기어코 나를 내려오게 만들려는 당신의 속마음이 헤아려지고도 남음이 있었다.

그런데 팔 년 세월에 비하면 김포공항에서 단 오십 분 만에 훌쩍 날아간 고향은 참으로 가까운 곳이었다. 기내에 퍼져 틀틀거리는 엔진 폭음에 귀가 먹먹해져서 잠시 멍한 방심 상태에서 몸을 맡기고 있는데 별안간 기체가 덜컹하기에 눈을 떠 보니 제주공항이었다는 식으로 나는 고향에 닿았다. 정말 눈 깜짝할 새에 고향땅 한복판에 뚝 떨어진 거였다. 그건 흡사 나 자신이 고향을 찾은 게 아니라 거꾸로 고향이 나를 찾아온 것처럼 어리둥절하고 낭패스러웠다. 뭐랄까, 아무 예비 감정도 없이 고향과 맞닥뜨린 셈이랄까. 나는 비행기 안에서 좀 진지하게 생각하지 못하고 멍하니 허송한 오십 분이 못내 후회스러웠다. 괜히 비행기를 탔다 싶었다. 기차를 타고 배를 타야 하는 건데 팔 년 만의 귀향을 직장 통근 시간에 불과한 단 오십 분에 끝내다니.

that not only covered the food for the annual service but also provided for housekeeping. However, my father's contribution didn't relieve my feelings of guilt for not being able to look after the ancestral burial ground or participate in the yearly memorial services. Eventually I ended up being summoned by my uncle. In his letter, he told me to come down for my grandfather's memorial day since he needed to discuss with me the purchase of our extended family's burial site. The tone of the letter made it more than clear that he was determined that I come this time.

Despite the eight years it took me to return, my hometown was just a fifty-minute flight from Gimp'o Airport. I had been in a daze for a moment, thanks to the deafening engine noise inside the airplane, when, startled by a sudden loud clunking sound coming from the fuselage, I opened my eyes and found myself at Jeju Airport. That was how I arrived. In the blink of an eye I was dropped right into the middle of my hometown, so to speak. It was disorienting and awkward, as if my hometown had come upon me, instead of me coming to visit the place. In other words, I was face to face with it without any emotional preparation. I deeply regret-

내게 고향이란 무엇이었나. 나에게 깊은 우울증과 찌든 가난밖에 남겨 준 것이 없는 곳이었다. 관광지니 어쩌니 하지만 그것도 지역 나름이어서 나의 향리인 서촌은 이렇다 할 관광자원도 없고 하늬바람이 몰아쳐 귤 농사도 안 되는 한촌이었다. 적어도 내 상상 속에서 나의 향리는 예나 제나 죽은 마을이었다. 말하자면 삼십 년 전 군 소개 작전에 따라 소각된 잿더미 모습 그대로 머리에 떠오르는 것이었다. 그래서 고향을 외면하여 살아오길 팔 년, 그 유맹의 십 년 전으로 되찾아 가려면 아무래도 조심스럽게 주저주저하며 다가가야 하리라. 기차를 타도 완행을 타서 반도 끝까지 가 거기서 다시 배를 타고 밤을 지새우며 밤 항해를 해야 하는 수륙 천오백 리 길. 차멀미, 뱃멀미에 시달리며 소주에 젖고 팔 년 만에 찾아가는 고향 생각에 젖어서 허위허위 찾아가야 할 고향이었다. 이것이 내가 평소에 고향을 지척에다 두고서도 지구 끝처럼 아득하게 여기던 이유였다.

그러나 휴가는 단 이틀이고 할아버지 제사가 바로 오늘인 걸 어떻게 하랴. 기차 타며 그렇게 여유작작하게 우회해서 고향에 갈 수는 없는 노릇이었다. 나는 마치 스튜어디스에게 등을 떠밀린 사람처럼 엉거주춤거리며 승강구

ted mindlessly wasting those fifty minutes that I should have spent in serious reflection. I shouldn't have flown, I thought. I should have taken a train and then a boat for a homecoming eight years overdue. The trip should have lasted longer than fifty minutes, which is my daily commuting time.

What did my hometown mean to me? It had given me nothing but profound depression and intractable poverty. The island itself may be a tourist destination, but the effects of tourism were uneven. In West Village, my birthplace, there were few if any tourist attractions. It was a desolate place where even tangerine trees, ubiquitous elsewhere on the island, couldn't grow because of the whipping west wind. At least in my mind it had always been lifeless. That is, I always remembered it as the piles of ash to which it had been reduced after the mandatory evacuation by the military thirty years ago. I should have realized that the way back to that place and time, after eight years of avoidance, after eight years of drifting in self-imposed exile, would require great care and caution on my part. Those 600 kilometers over land and water should have been covered by the slowest train to the tip of the peninsula, followed by the overnight ferry. I would have been

계단을 내려왔다.

하늘은 낮은 구름에 덮여 음울해 보였고 한라산 정상은 구름 떼가 잔뜩 몰려 있었다. 낯익은 제주도 특유의 겨울 날씨였다. 그건 어린 시절의 겨울 하늘을 낮게 덮고 벗겨질 줄 모르던 바로 그 음울한 구름이었다. 흐린 날씨 때문에 돌담은 더 검고 딱딱해 보이고 한라산 기슭의 질펀한 목장에 덮인 눈빛은 침침했다. 하늬바람이 불어와 귓가에 달라붙어 떨어지지 않는 바람 소리, 쉴 새 없이 고시랑거리는 앞 머리칼. 나는 불현듯 가슴이 답답해 왔다. 어린 시절의 그 음울한 겨울철로 돌아온 것이었다.

나는 동문 로터리에서 내 향리인 서촌을 경유하는 버스를 탔다. 시골행 차는 온통 고향 사투리로 왁자지껄했다.

"할마니, 이거 뭐우꽈?" 하고 남자 차장이 통로에 부려 놓은 대 구덕(바구니) 속의 옹기 허벅을 가리켰다.

"아따, 팥죽이라 팥죽. 팥죽 쑤언 삼양 동네에 고렴감서." 광목 수건을 쓰고 눈이 짓무른 할머니가 구덕에 달린 질빵을 쥔 채 대답했다.

참으로 오랜만에 듣는 고향 사투리였다. 내 입가에도 은연중에 고향 사투리가 떠올라 뱅뱅 맴돌았다.

버스는 계속 털털거리면서 해변 따라 일주 도로를 타고

worn out by motion sickness, soaked in *soju,* and drenched in nostalgia. Because it was that kind of hometown, I always felt it was at the ends of the earth even though it was in reality just a stone's throw away.

But I had only two days off and my grandfather's memorial day was today. A leisurely detour by train and all hadn't been an option. I descended the stairway from the plane hesitantly, as if being pushed by the flight attendant.

The sky, overcast with low-hanging clouds, looked melancholy, and heavy clusters of cumulus gathered around the peak of Mt. Halla. There was that familiar winter climate, distinctive of the island. There were the same ominous and persistent clouds that never peeled off my childhood sky. The cloudy sky made the stone walls look darker and harder than usual and caused the snow on the marshy meadow around the base of Mt. Halla to appear dull. The howling of the west wind clung to the rims of my ears. Strands of hair were murmuring incessantly across my forehead. All of a sudden I felt heaviness in my chest. I was back to the dismal winters of my childhood.

At the East Gate rotary, I got on a bus that would

달려갔다. 일상생활에 노상 모래바람이 부는 어촌들. 헌 그물로 바람에 날아가지 않게 단도리해 놓은 초가집 추녀. 돌담 울타리 너머 바람에 부대끼는 빨간 열매 달린 사철나무들. 나는 내 눈이 육지서 온 관광객의 호기심 많은 눈이 안 되도록 조심하면서 이것저것 눈여겨보았다.

잿빛 바다 안으로 날카롭게 먹혀들어간 시커먼 현무암의 갑, 저걸 사투리로 '코지'라고 했지. 바닷가 넓은 '돌빌레'에 높직이 쌓여 있는 저 고동색 해초 더미는 '듬북눌'이겠고, 겨울 바다에 포말처럼 둥둥 떠 있는 저것들은 해녀들의 '태왁'이다. 시커먼 현무암 바위 틈바구니에 붉게 타는 조짚불, 뭍에 오른 해녀들의 불을 쬐는 저곳을 '불턱'이라고 했지. 나는 잊어 먹고 있던 낱말들이 심층 의식 깊은 데서 하나하나 튀어나올 때마다 남모르는 쾌재를 불렀다. 이렇게 추억의 심부로 들어가면 들어갈수록 내 머릿속은 고향의 풍물과 사투리로 그들먹해지는 것이었다.

그날은 하루에 두 집 제사라 큰당숙 댁에서 종조모 제사를 초저녁에 먼저 치른 다음 모두 큰집에 모였다. 나는 누구보다도 길수 형을 만나는 것이 즐거웠다. 나와는 겨우 한 살 차이인데도 벗어진 이마 태깔이 벌써 중년 티가 완연했다. 그는 요즘 귤 밭을 하나 일구노라고 중학교에

stop at my native West Village. This country-bound bus was bursting with the boisterous island dialect.

"Grandma, what's in this?" the male bus attendant asked, pointing at a dark, brown-glazed earthenware pot in a bamboo basket plunked down in the aisle.

"Ah, it's red-bean porridge. You see, I made it to take to a memorial service in Samyang Village," said a bleary-eyed grandma with a cotton hanky wrapped around her head, the shoulder strap of the basket still in her grip.

It had been a really long time since I last heard my hometown vernacular. Before I knew it, native idioms were floating up to my lips and lingering there.

The bus continued rattling along the coastal road that looped around the island. In fishing villages accustomed to relentless sandy wind, the eaves of thatched roofs were secured with old fishing nets. Beyond the stone walls, evergreens with red berries were enduring the gusts. Guarding myself agains becoming another curious tourist from the mainland, I was taking in the various sights we passed.

A pitch-black whinstone promontory was sinking its sharp teeth into the charcoal-colored sea. Such a

서 받는 봉급의 절반이 날아간다고 했다.

생각했던 대로 인사 올릴 만한 친척 어른들은 모두 참례하고 있어서 짧은 일정에 일일이 찾아다니는 번거로움을 피할 수 있어 좋았다. 제주시에 사는 고모 식구들은 밤늦어 차편으로 도착했다. 부쩍 늙어 버린 친척 어른들의 얼굴을 대하자니 그동안 찾아뵙지 못한 팔 년이란 세월이 실감으로 가슴에 와 닿는 것이었다. 흰 머리칼에 대조되어 얼굴에 핀 검버섯이 더욱 뚜렷하게 돋보이는 큰아버지, 주름진 눈에 항시 눈물이 질펵한 큰당숙어른. 나는 각오했던 대로 한참 고개를 숙이고 어른들의 책망을 다소곳이 들었다. 그러고 나서 서울서 아내 몰래 좀 무리해서 마련한 봉투 삼만 원짜리 석 장과 이만 원짜리 다섯 장을 내놓았다. 팔 년 만에 귀향하는 서울의 큰 회사의 부장에 대한 고향 친척들의 기대감을 도무지 저버릴 수가 없었던 것이다. 봉투를 내밀면서, 물건으로 사올까도 생각했지만 어떤 게 필요한 물건인지 몰라서 좀 뭣하지만 그냥 돈으로 드리니 양해해 달라는 말을 덧붙이기를 잊지 않았다. 그런데 다른 분들이야 현금이 귀한 농촌 생활이라 돈 봉투는 충분히 생색이 나겠지만 도청 주사로 있으면서 밀감밭도 꽤 크게 갖고 있는 고모부에게마저 봉투를 내밀자니

formation was called *k'oji* in our dialect. Those heaping piles of auburn seaweed on the broad *tol-billae* rocks on the shore must be *tŭmbungnul*, and what looked like bubbles of foam floating on the winter sea were the *t'aewak* of women divers. The red blazing from cracks in the dark whinstone was a bonfire of millet straw, and the fireplace where women divers would warm themselves when they emerged from the water was called *pult'ŏk*. I gave a silent cheer each time a forgotten word burst from the depths of my subconsciousness. The deeper I dug into the core of my memories, the more my mind bustled with the scenery and dialect of my native home.

Since there were two memorial services in two households that day, the extended family performed an early evening service for Great Aunt at Older Tangsuk's place and then congregated at Older Uncle's place. I was especially delighted to get together again with my older cousin Kil-su. Though he was only a year older than me, middle age had already set in: his hairline was receding. He told me that he was spending over half his salary as a middle school teacher to clear a plot of land for tangerine trees.

좀 쑥스러운 느낌이 들었다. 아닌게 아니라, 고모부는 한마디 능청떨어 내 얼굴을 화끈 달게 하기를 잊지 않았다.

"이게 뭐라? 욕을 그만해 달라고 와이로 씀이라? 하이고, 나도 이런저런 와이로 다 먹어 봤쥬만 처조캐한티 와이로 얻어먹긴 이거 처음인디……."

고모부는 이 지방 사투리를 수월수월 잘도 말했다. 평안도 용강 사투리를 영 못 버리던 저분이 이젠 깔축없이 제주도 사람이 되었구나. 서북청년으로 입도해서 이제 삼십 년도 넘고 있으니 충분히 그럴 만도 하리라.

대개 초저녁에 잠자 버릇해서 제삿날이면 노상 꾸벅꾸벅 졸기를 잘하는 시골 어른들이었지만 그날은 나를 맞아 자정이 넘도록 이야기꽃을 피웠다.

가족 장지 매입에 대한 의논을 끝내고 이 이야기 저 이야기 한담을 즐기고 있는데 불현듯 순이삼촌 생각이 났다. 아까부터 그분이 보이지 않는 게 이상했다. 어릴 때 보면 큰집 제삿날마다 부주로 기주떡 구덕을 들고 오던 분이었다. 촌수는 멀어도 서너 집 건너 이웃에 살아서 큰집과는 서로 기제사에 왕래할 정도로 각별한 사이였던 것이다. 그래서 길수 형과 나는 어려서부터 그분을 삼촌이라고 부르면서 무척 따랐다(고향에서는 촌수 따지기 어려

As I had anticipated, almost all the elderly relatives I was obliged to pay my respects to were present, and thankfully I could avoid having to visit them individually under such time pressure. My aunt's family had driven from Jeju City, arriving in the middle of the night. The remarkable signs of aging on their faces made me acutely aware of my eight-year absence. The dark blotches on Older Uncle's face stood out in sharp contrast to his white hair. Older Tangsuk's chronically watery eyes were surrounded by wrinkles. For a while, I hung my head low and accepted their admonitions without protest. I had expected as much. Then I presented them with eight envelopes, three with 30,000 *wŏn* and five with 20,000 *wŏn*—beyond my means—that I had prepared without consulting my wife. It was impossible to disregard the expectations my hometown relatives must have had of a big corporate executive from Seoul who was returning home after eight years. Presenting the envelopes, I didn't forget to apologize for my poor taste in offering cash and add that I had thought of buying gifts but couldn't figure out what specifically they would need. The envelopes were most likely to be thoroughly appreciated by cash-strapped country folk, except for my

운 먼 친척 어른을 남녀 구별 없이 흔히 삼촌이라 불러 가까이 지내는 풍습이 있다). 어서 삼촌을 찾아뵙고 인사를 드려야 할 텐데. 더구나 삼촌은 일 년 가까이 서울 우리 집에 올라와 밥을 해 주며 고생하다가 불과 두 달 전에 내려오셨는데 그동안 어떻게 지내고 계신지 퍽 궁금했다. 혹시 몸이 편찮으신 게 아닐까? 나는 길수 형에게 물어보았다.

"형, 순이삼촌이 통 안 보염싱게 무슨 일이 이서?"

그런데 웬일인지 내 말에 사람들은 하던 말을 문득 멈추고 조용해졌다. 길수 형의 얼굴에 난처한 기색이 역력하게 떠올랐다. 큰아버지도 나와 시선이 마주치자 입맛을 쩝쩝 다시며 얼굴을 돌렸다. 잠시 방 안은 안쓰런 침묵이 흘렀다. 왜들 이러실까? 나이 스물여섯에 홀어머니 되어 삼십 년이란 긴긴 세월을 수절해 오던 순이삼촌이 지금에 와서 개가라도 했단 말인가? 이윽고 큰아버지가 담뱃재를 화로 운두에 털면서 고개를 들어 나를 건너다보았다.

"겨를 없어 너한티는 못 알렸져마는 그 삼춘은 며칠 전에 죽어 부러시네."

"아니, 그게 무슨 말씀이우꽈? 순이삼춘이 돌아가셔서 마씸?"

paternal aunt's husband, a junior official in the provincial government who also owns a sizable tangerine field. I felt a bit embarrassed handing him an envelope, and sure enough he wasn't about to pass up an opportunity to humiliate me with his sarcasm.

"What's this? A bribe to stop us from badmouthing you? Man, I've taken all sorts of bribes but not from you until now..."

He spoke the local dialect with such ease. The guy who once seemed stuck with his accent from Yonggang in Pyŏngan Province could now easily pass as a native of Jeju Island. This was to be expected given the thirty plus years since he had come to the island as a member of the Northwest Youth Corps.

The country elders, who would typically doze through memorial services since they were used to going to bed early in the evening, took pleasure in talking with me past midnight that day.

We were wiling away the time chatting about various things after our discussion about purchasing a burial site for the extended family, when abruptly I thought of Sun-i Samch'on. Oddly, this aunt of mine had been missing all evening. I had childhood memories of her coming to every memorial service

그분이 돌아가시다니, 나는 어안이 벙벙할 따름이었다. 불과 두 달 전만 해도 잔병치레 없이 늘 정정하시던 분이 아니던가. 나는 도무지 믿기지 않아서 좌중을 휘둘러보았다. 작은당숙이 나에게 가만히 고개를 끄덕여 보였다.

"나도 몰랐는디 형님, 무사 나헌티는 기별도 안 합디가?"

이렇게 고모부가 말해도 큰아버지는 담배만 풀썩풀썩 피워댈 뿐 도무지 입을 열지 않았다. 평소에 친누이같이 지내던 사이인지라 몹시 괴로운 모양이었다. 좌중은 한참 침묵이 흘렀다. 싸르락, 싸르락. 창호지창에 싸락눈 흩뿌리는 소리가 들려왔다.

이윽고 큰아버지는 지그시 감았던 눈을 뜨고 나를 이윽히 바라보았다.

"그런 죽음은 몰라 좋은 거쥬만 일단 알았이니까 내일 서울 올라가기 전에 문상이나 해영 가라. 시에 딸네 집에 위패 모셨져." 하고 잠시 말을 끊었던 큰아버지는 새로 피워 문 담배를 깊이 들이마시고는 다시 말을 이었다.

"허기사 이래 죽으나 저래 죽으나 죽기는 매한가지쥬만……."

이렇게 떠듬떠듬 시작한 큰아버지의 얘기는 대강 이러

at Older Uncle's place with a pot of *kiju* rice cake as her contribution. Having lived just a few houses away in the neighborhood, she was on special terms with Older Uncle's family, so they attended each other's memorial services though they were not closely related. Quite naturally, Cousin Kil-su and I developed a deep affection for her from early childhood. We would call her Samch'on since it was customary in our village to designate distant but friendly relatives by this unisex title. I was looking forward to paying a visit and checking in on her. I was all the more anxious to find out how she had been since she had come back from Seoul just two months before after having endured a tough time helping my family with the cooking and housekeeping for almost a year. Maybe she wasn't feeling well? I asked Cousin Kil-su,

"*Cousin.* I haven't seen Sun-i Samch'on all evening. What's going on?"

Somehow my question put a damper on the conversations and everyone fell silent. Cousin Kil-su's expression betrayed his discomfort. When our eyes met, Older Uncle also turned away, clucking his tongue. An empathetic silence hung in the room for a moment. Why were they reacting like this? Did

했다.

그분은 돌아가신 날짜도 분명치 않았다. 집을 나간 날이 곧 당신이 돌아가신 날이 되겠는데 그걸 아는 사람이 아무도 없었다. 그럴 수밖에 없는 것이, 하나 있는 딸자식을 시집보낸 후 여러 해 홀몸으로 살아오던 터라 당신이 먼저 말하지 않으면 밥을 끓이는지 죽을 쑤는지 이웃에선 도무지 알 길이 없었다.

처음 며칠은 집이 덧문까지 닫혀 있는 걸 보고 딸네 집에 갔겠거니 하고 예사로 생각했었다. 그런데 딸네 집에 가도 자고 오는 법이 없이 그날로 돌아오곤 하던 분이 보름이 넘도록 보이지 않자 큰집에선 차차 불길스럽게 생각되었다. 또 서울 조카네 집(우리 집)에 갔나? 서울 가면 간다고 말했을 텐데. 걱정된 나머지 큰집 식구들은 시에 있는 딸네 집에다 연락했다. 딸과 사위가 달려와 당신이 있을 만한 곳을 이곳저곳 찾아다녔다. 전에 신경쇠약으로 몇 개월 정양했던 한라산 밑 절간에도 가 보았다. 파래나 톳을 뜯으러 갔다가 무슨 횡액을 만났나 하고 바닷가 바위 틈서리도 뒤졌다.

그러다가 결국 당신은 국민학교 근처 일주 도로변의 밭에서 시체로 발견되었는데 부패한 정도로 봐서 죽은 지

she finally find a new husband or some such thing after remaining chaste for thirty long years since she became a widow with small children at the age of twenty-six? It wasn't long before my uncle, knocking the ashes from his cigarette on the rim of the open charcoal stove, looked up and across at me.

"So busy with things we didn't get around to notifying you, but *Samch'on* died a few days ago."

"Wait a minute, what are you saying? Sun-i Samch'on passed away?"

Hearing so unexpectedly that she had died, I was simply dumbfounded. Until two months ago she seemed hale and hearty without even minor complaints. In disbelief, I looked around at everyone in the room. Younger Tangsuk gave me a quiet nod.

"I wasn't aware either, *Older Brother.* How come I wasn't informed?" My paternal aunt's husband protested, too, but my uncle just kept puffing away on his cigarette without a word. He was obviously in tremendous anguish over the fate of someone who was practically a real sister to him. Everyone was silent for a while. *Ssarŭrak, ssarŭrak.* We could hear small pellets of dry snow hitting the window paper.

Finally my uncle's gently closed eyes opened and

이십 일은 좋이 넘어 보였다. 그 밭이 일주 도로에서 한 발 건너에 있었음에도 이십 일이 넘도록 사람 눈에 안 띈 것은 거기가 후미지고 옴팡진 밭인데다 밭담으로 가리어 있었기 때문이다. 게다가 흰옷 아닌 밤색 두루마기를 입고 있어서 더더욱 눈에 안 띄었을 것이다. 서울 우리 집에 올라올 때 입었던 밤색 두루마기에 따뜻한 토끼털 목도리까지 두르고 자는 듯 모로 누워 있었다. 머리맡에는 먹다 남은 꿩 약 사이나가 몇 알갱이 흩어져 있고…… 그렇게 발견된 것이 불과 여드레 전이라는 것이었다.

"나도 따라가 봤우다만, 거참 이상헌 일도 다 있십디다. 그사이 눈이 나련 보리밭이 사뭇 해영허게(하얗게) 눈이 덮였는디 말이우다, 참 이상허게시리 순이삼촌 누운 자리만 눈이 녹안 있지 않애여 마씸" 하고 육촌 현모 형이 말하자 큰아버지가 맞장구쳤다.

"발복헐 땅이여. 그 동생이 죽어도 자기가 드러누울 묏자리 하나는 잘 잡았쥬."

"발복해 봐사 무슨 자손이 있어야쥬. 외손편엔 몰라도…… 양자 들이라, 들이라, 경(그렇게) 말해도 노시(영) 말을 안 들엉게(듣더니만) 쯧쯧." 하고 큰당숙어른들이 애석하다는 듯 혀를 찼다.

lifted with a serene look toward me.

"Such a death would be better for you not to know about. However, now that you do, you should pay a visit to the deceased and the surviving family before going back to Seoul tomorrow. Her mortuary plaque is at her daughter's place in the city." After pausing briefly and drawing deeply on a new cigarette, he continued.

"At any rate, we all die one way or another, but..."

The story he so reluctantly started to tell was roughly as follows.

First of all, even the date of her death was unknown. No one knew what day she disappeared, though it could have served as her proper memorial day. This wasn't surprising, though, since she had lived by herself for years after her daughter, her only child, married and moved away. Her neighbors had no way of knowing what was cooking in her house unless she voluntarily told them.

For the first few days, her neighbors noticed that the outer door of her house remained shut but they did not give it much thought, assuming she must be visiting her daughter in the city. However, Older Uncle's family grew apprehensive when they real-

이야기를 듣고 있는 동안 내 등에는 남모르는 식은땀이 흘러내렸다. 얼마 동안 귀가 먹먹해지고 말소리가 들리지 않았다. 한평생 다 산 나이 쉰여섯에 끔찍하게도 스스로 목숨을 끊다니. 평생 일궈 먹던 밭을 찾아가 양지바른 데를 골라 드러누워 버린 삼촌, 유서도 한 장 없이 죽었으니 그것은 표면상 아무 뚜렷한 이유가 없는 죽음이었다. 그렇다. 정신이 잘못되어 죽었다는 큰아버지의 판단이 옳을 것이다. 평소의 지병인 신경쇠약이 원인이 되었으리라. 그런데 신경쇠약은 왜 갑자기 악화되었을까? 거기에는 어떤 계기가 있을 것이다. 무엇이 삼촌을 죽음의 궁지로까지 몰아붙였나? 혹시 항상 원만치 못했던 일 년 동안의 서울 우리 집 생활에서 병이 악화된 게 아닐까? 아니, 그럴리 없어. 여기 내려와서 무슨 충격적인 일을 당해도 당했을 테지. 그런데 친척 어른들의 얘기는 고향에 내려와서는 이렇다 할 사고가 없었다는 것이었다. 게다가 서울 우리 집에서 내려온 지 한 달도 채 못되어 일어난 일이고…… 가책과 후회의 감정으로 나는 가슴이 오그라 붙는 듯했다.

생각하면 순이삼촌이 우리 집에 와 있었던 지난 일 년은 당신이나 나나 내 아내나 모두 서로가 불편스럽고 원

ized she hadn't been seen for over two weeks. She rarely stayed anywhere overnight, even at her daughter's place. Did she return to her nephew's in Seoul? She would have let them know if she had. Alarmed, Older Uncle's family contacted her daughter in the city. Her daughter and son-in-law rushed here and started looking for her in the most likely places. They checked the Buddhist temple at the foot of Mt. Halla where Sun-i Samch'on once spent several months recuperating from a nervous breakdown. They searched between the rocks on the shore in case she had fallen victim to disaster while collecting sea lettuce or green laver.

Eventually her body was found in a field adjacent to the loop road that runs by the elementary school. The state of decomposition indicated that she had died at least twenty days before. Though there was only another patch between this particular field and the road, her body escaped being spotted as long as it did because the field was not only tucked away and depressed but also concealed behind walls marking the boundaries between the patches of land. Moreover, she was in a traditional overcoat that was brown instead of white, which made it harder to notice her. She was lying on her side, as if

만치 못했던 게 사실이었다. 아내가 벌이도 시원찮은 옷가게를 진작 걷어치웠더라면 삼촌이 올라오지 않아도 되었을 텐데. 그러나 하루 종일 아내가 의상실에 매달려 있는 형편이니 밥해 주는 사람이 따로 있지 않으면 안 되었다. 재작년 일 년 동안 밥하는 여자아이들이 서너 차례 불나게 엇갈려 들락거리더니, 나중에는 그나마 구하기가 무척 어려워졌다. 그래서 길수 형에게 편지를 내어 고향에다 수소문해 봤던 것인데, 마침 순이삼촌이 서울 구경도 해볼 겸 우리 집에 한 일 년 와 있겠다고 나섰던 것이었다.

순이삼촌이 손잡이가 망가진 옷가방을 질빵으로 짊어지고 우리 집에 온 지 열흘도 못되어 언짢은 일이 발생했다. 아내가 가게에서 아직 돌아오지 않은 저녁때였다. 당신은 잔뜩 굳은 표정으로 내 방으로 건너왔다.

"조캐, 참말 이럴 수가 이싱가?"

삼촌의 눈에선 눈물마저 글썽거리고 있었다. 무슨 일일까? 나는 영문도 모르고 가슴이 섬뜩했다.

"아니, 무슨 일이 있었어요? 여기 앉아서 자초지종을 얘기해 보세요."

평소에 순이삼촌 앞에서는 고향 말을 써야지 하고 생각하던 터라 무의식중에 툭 튀어나온 서울말이 무척 민망스

asleep, in the very same overcoat and warm rabbit-fur scarf she was wearing when she came to Seoul to stay with my family. Left scattered beside her head were some cyanide pills often used by pheasant hunters.... It was only eight days earlier that she had been found this way.

"I followed the others to check it out. It was indeed a peculiar thing to see. While the barley field was mostly white from a recent snowfall, the snow was strangely melted at the spot where Sun-i Samch'on lay," Second Cousin Hyŏn-mo said.

Older Uncle chimed in, "That piece of land is going to change her family's luck. Even in the face of death, that little sister of mine picked a good spot for her own burial and laid herself down there."

"What good is a change in fortune when there's no heir to the family name? Unless her daughter's child counts... We tried many times to talk her into adopting a son but she wouldn't listen, *tsk tsk*," other elder uncles added with regret.

A cold sweat secretly trickled down my spine as I listened to the story. For a while my ears felt plugged up, and the voices around me sounded muffled. How ghastly that she ended her own life at the ripe old age of fifty-six, toward the end of her lifetime.

러웠다.

"동네 사람들이 날 숭보암서라. 새로 온 민기네 집 식모는 밥 하영(많이) 먹는 제주도 할망(할미)이엔 소문나서라."

나는 하도 말도 안 되는 말이라 어이가 없었다.

"아니, 누게가 그런 쓸데없는 소릴 협디가?"

"허기사 고향서 궂은일, 쌍일을 허멍(하면서) 보리밥 한 사발 고봉으로 먹던 버릇 따문에 아멍(아무리) 밥을 적게 먹젱 해도 공기밥 먹는 조캐네들보다사 하영 먹어지는 게 사실이쥬. 사실이 그렇댄 해도 밥 하영 먹는 식모엔 사방팔방에 논(남)한티 소문내는 벱이 어디 이시니?"

나는 순간 눈망울이 확 더워지면서 눈물이 핑 돌았다. 삼촌보고 밥 많이 먹는 식모라니, 이런 모욕적인 언사가 도대체 어디 있단 말인가. 나도 분통이 터져 견딜 수 없었다.

"누게가 그런 말을 협디가? 어디서 들입디가?"

그러나 삼촌은 치맛귀로 눈물을 찍어낼 뿐 통 대답을 하지 않았다.

"민기 어멍(엄마)이 그런 말을 협디가? 어디 말해 봅서. 요 아래 희야네 가게서 그런 말을 협디가? 꼭 밝혀내서 혼

Samch'on chose the field that she had tilled for her entire life and decided to lie down on its sunny side. With no suicide note left behind, it was on the surface a suicide with no clear reason. So it had to be a death from mental illness, as my uncle declared. It must have been caused by her chronic neurosis. Anyway, what set off such an abrupt decline? There must have been a trigger. What cornered Samch'on and left her with no choice but death? Was it perhaps that unpleasant year she spent with us in Seoul that exacerbated her illness? No, it couldn't have been. Something traumatic must have happened to her after she came back here. However, the elderly relatives couldn't recall her having any episode to speak of after she returned home. Besides, it happened less than a month after she returned from Seoul... I felt my heart being crushed by guilt and remorse.

Looking back, I realized that the year Sun-i Samch'on spent with my family was indeed an uncomfortable and uneasy time not only for her but also for me and my wife. If my wife had given up her not-so-lucrative clothing business sooner, Samch'on wouldn't have had to come up to Seoul. As it was, my wife was tied to her dress shop all day long,

을 내사 허쿠다. 혼저(어서) 말해 봅서.”

그러나 삼촌은 여전히 대답을 하지 않았다. 그래도 내가 붉으락푸르락 화를 내는 것에 다소 위안을 얻었는지는 몰라도 삼촌은 더 이상 따져 들지 않고 그만 물러갔다.

아내가 그런 말을 했나? 설마하니 아내가 그런 희떠운 언동을 할 경박한 여자일까? 혹시 민기 놈이 희야네 가게에 군것질하러 갔다가 그런 못된 말을 했을지도 모른다. 아니, 다섯 살짜리 숫기도 없는 녀석이 어떻게 그런 당돌한 말을 해? 그러나 '밥 많이 먹는 제주도 식모'라고 말했을 리는 없지만 밥 많이 먹는다는 말은 누가 해도 했을 것이다. 이런 의심이 좀처럼 풀리지 않은 채 저녁 늦게 돌아온 아내를 맞고 보니 자연히 말다툼이 벌어졌다. 내가 전에 없이 치를 떨며 화를 내는 꼴을 보고 놀랐던지 아내는 결혼 후 처음으로 내 앞에서 눈물을 보였다. 나는 격앙된 어조로, 시부모 없어 시집살이를 면하더니 시댁 어른을 대하는 게 도무지 버릇없다고 질타했던 것이다. 하여간 아내가 그런 말을 했고 안 했고 간에, 그날 밤 나는 아내가 순이삼촌 앞에서 어떻게 처신해야 할지를 내 딴에는 톡톡히 보여 준 셈이었다.

밥을 좀 많이 드신다고 해서, 누구나 건져내 버리는 배

which left us with no choice but to have a housekeeper. During the previous year, we went through three or four housemaids, one right after another, like a revolving door. After that, it was difficult to find even short-term domestic help. It was then that I wrote to Cousin Kil-su asking him if anyone in my hometown might be interested, and Sun-i Samch'on happened to volunteer to help us out for a year or so while experiencing life in Seoul.

Not even ten days after Sun-i Samch'on showed up, a suitcase with a broken handle strapped on her back, something disheartening happened. It was evening and my wife wasn't home from work yet. Sam-chon came to my room with a tense face.

"Nephew, how could you do this to me?"

Her eyes were welling up. What on earth happened? My heart sank, though I didn't know why.

"Oh no, did something happen to you? Please sit down and tell me what happened."

I felt terribly apologetic about my unchecked Seoul accent, for I had been careful to use our hometown dialect in her presence.

"The neighbors are whispering behind my back. The rumor's going around that the new kitchen maid for Min-gi's family's is an old lady from Jeju

춧국의 멸치를 잡수신다고 해서, 잘 통하지 않는 사투리를 쓴다고 해서 그게 어째 흉이 된단 말인가. 시골에 혼자 먹고살 만큼은 농토도 있고 남을 빌려 주고 온 오막살이지만 집도 있는 분이었다. 말 그대로 서울 구경할 겸해서 우리 집 일을 도우러 오신 분을 흉보다니. 아내의 태도가 우선 글러 먹었다. 순이삼촌이 하는 사투리를 아내는 알아듣지 못했다. 이해해 보려고 애쓰는 것 같지도 않았다. 저게 무슨 말이냐는 듯이 고개를 돌려 나를 바라볼 때 나는 나 자신이 무시당한 것처럼 얼굴이 붉어지는 것을 느껴야만 했다. 그건 신혼 초에 아내가 무슨 일로 호적초본을 뗐다가 제 본적이 남편 본적인 제주도로 올라 있는 당연한 사실을 가지고 무척 놀란 표정을 지었을 때 내가 느낀 수치감과 비슷한 것이었다. 이렇게 사투리를 알아듣지 못하는 아내 앞에서 순이삼촌의 처신은 어떻게 해야 옳은가? 그저 말수를 줄이고 시키는 말만 고분고분 따르는 수동적인 입장을 취할 도리밖에 더 있는가.

그날 이후 나는 여태 막연히 기피증 현상으로만 나타나던 고향에 대한 선입견을 대폭 수정하기로 했다. 삼촌의 존재가 나에게 늘 고향을 의식하게 해 준 셈이었다. 서울 생활 십오 년 동안 한 번도 써 보지 못하고 묵혀 두었던

Island who eats like a bottomless pit."

My jaw just dropped at the absurdity of this.

"Huh? Who's spreading such a ridiculous story?"

"Well, it's true that I end up chomping more than you folks who use such tiny bowls for rice. No matter how hard I try to cut down, I'm still used to having a heaping bowl full of rice, a habit from my days of tough manual labor back home. Even if it's true, you shouldn't have spread such gossip about the housemaid with a huge appetite all around the neighborhood."

At that moment, I felt blood rushing to my eyes and making them brim with tears. Samch'on was being called a kitchen maid who eats like a pig. What an intolerable insult. I could hardly bear my own indignation.

"Who told you that? Where did you hear it?"

Samch'on just dabbed at her tears with a corner of her skirt, not answering.

"Did Min-gi's mom say anything like that? Please tell me. Was it anyone at Hŭi-ya's convenience store down the street? I'll get to the bottom of this and make sure the culprit pays dearly. Come on, please, who was it?"

Samch'on still refused to say. Whether or not my

사투리도 쓰기 시작했다. 고향 말은 주로 삼촌하고 얘기할 때만 썼지만 민기 놈에게도 사투리를 꽤나 많이 가르쳐 주었다. 그렇다. 나는 내 아들이 허여멀끔한 아내를 닮아 빈틈없이 서울내기가 되어 가는 것이 딱 질색이었다. 에미를 닮아선지, TV를 너무 봐선지, 다섯 살 나이에 벌써 안경을 써야 할 지경으로 눈이 나쁜 녀석, 아내는 피아노를 가르쳐 줄 계획이지만 나는 녀석에게 투박한 고향 사투리를 가르치고 싶었다. 아들놈마저 제 애비의 고향을 외면할 수는 없는 일이었다. 그렇다. 서울말 일변도의 내 언어생활이란 게 얼마나 가식적이고 억지춘향식이었던가. 그건 어디까지나 표절 인생이지 나 자신의 인생은 아니었다.

그러나 순이삼촌은 그때 일로 퍽 상심했던지 좀처럼 밝은 표정으로 돌아오지 않았다. 거의 말도 하지 않았다. 그렇게 용서를 빌었는데도 삼촌은 삭이지 않고 내내 꼬불쳐 두고 있는 모양이었다. 드디어 아내와 정면으로 맞부딪치고 말았다.

어느 날 회사일로 저녁 늦게 귀가해 보니 삼촌과 아내가 말다툼하고 있었다. 삼촌은 나를 보자 울면서 부엌 바닥에 주저앉아 버리는 것이었다. 나는 무슨 일이냐고 아

obvious fury had placated her to some extent, she stopped protesting and withdrew from the room.

Did my wife start this gossip? She wasn't so shallow as to make frivolous remarks, or was she? Maybe little Min-gi said something disrespectful like that when he was at Hŭi-ya's store for candy. But could a bashful five-year-old utter such audacious words? The bottom line was, somebody must have mentioned Samch'on's unusually big appetite, even if they didn't exactly call her that "ravenous kitchen-maid from Jeju Island." I had been brooding over these unresolved suspicions when my wife came home late from work, so it was only natural that we got into an argument. Probably shaken that I was gnashing my teeth with anger as never before, she broke down in tears in front of me for the first time since we got married. In the excitement, I accused her of being disrespectful to her elderly in-law because she had never lived with in-law parents who would have taught her how to behave. Whether or not she was the culprit, I did my best that night to make sure my wife understood how to conduct herself with Sun-i Samch'on.

So what if she had an appetite bigger than normal, or ate the anchovies others usually pick out of cab-

내에게 눈을 부라렸다. 그러자 이번엔 아내가 눈물을 주르륵 흘리는 게 아닌가, 빌어먹을.

아내는 순이삼촌이 쌀이 다 떨어져서 사와야 한다는 말에 "쌀이 벌써 떨어졌어요?"라고 예사로 말을 던졌을 뿐이란다. 알았다는 뜻에서, 아, 그래요? 하듯이 가볍게 한 말을, 서울말의 억양에 익숙하지 못해서 그랬던지 "쌀이 벌써 다 떨어질 리가 있나요?" 하는 반문으로 잘못 이해했다는 것이었다. 그래서 삼촌은, 내가 너무 밥을 많이 먹어서 쌀이 일찍 떨어진 줄 아느냐, 도둑년처럼 내가 쌀을 몰래 내다 팔았다는 말이냐, 하면서 우는 것이었다. 참 기가 찰 노릇이었다. 하도 어이없는 일이라 어디서 어떻게 수습해야 좋을지 몰랐다. 다만, 하잘것없는 일에 꼼짝없이 붙잡혀 상심하고 있는 삼촌을 보자 나 자신 눈시울이 뜨거워지는 것이었다.

그날 우리 내외는 오해를 풀어 안심시켜 드리려고 얼마나 애를 썼던가. 그러나 그게 아무 소용도 없었음이 그 뒤부터 노출된 삼촌의 야릇한 결벽증에서 판명되었다. 쌀이 일찍 떨어진 원인이 밥을 질게 하거나 눌게 한 데 있다고 그 나름대로 판단했던지 순이삼촌은 그 뒤부터 된밥을 지어 내려고 무진 신경을 쓰는 눈치였다. 된밥을 만드는 일

bage soup, or spoke in a dialect incomprehensible to us? How could she be faulted for any of those acts? She wasn't entirely without means, either. Back home, she had enough farmland to support herself, and a house, though modest, that she rented out. She came to Seoul quite literally to help us with housekeeping while enjoying the attractions of the city. She didn't deserve any disparaging remarks. My wife had the wrong attitude from the start. She couldn't understand Sun-i Samch'on's dialect at all. And she didn't seem to make any effort to do so. Every time she turned to me, as if asking me to agree that Samch'on was speaking gibberish, I couldn't help blushing as if her contempt were directed at me. This was akin to the humiliation I had felt early in our marriage when my wife obtained a copy of our family registry for some reason and seemed astonished at the logical fact that her permanent address was now the same as mine, Jeju Island. How was Sun-i Samch'on supposed to conduct herself around my wife who couldn't even comprehend her dialect? Other than speaking as little as possible and submissively following instructions, that is.

이 무슨 지독한 강박관념처럼 삼촌을 짓누르고 있었다. 때문에 위 무력 증세가 있어 진밥을 좋아하는 나였지만 쓰다 궂다 한마디 말도 할 수 없었다. 게다가 쌀 사온 지 열흘도 못되어 그동안 얼마나 먹었는지 알아내려고 하루 종일 됫박질해 보는 모습은 정말 애처롭다 못해 섬뜩한 느낌마저 주는 것이었다.

이렇게 비슷한 일을 두 번 겪고 난 다음부터는 아내는 또 순이삼촌의 오해를 살까 봐 언동을 조심하느라고 거의 신경과민이 될 지경이었다. 내가 보기에도 아내의 삼촌에 대한 태도는 크게 달라져 있었다. 그러나 삼촌은 뚱하게 굳어진 표정이 풀릴 날이 없었다. 심지어는 나에게마저 말하기를 기피하는 눈치가 역력했다. 공원에 놀러 가서 사진을 서너 장 찍어 드렸는데 사진값을 내겠다고 우기지를 않나, 토마토 주스를 들면서 같이 들자고 권해도 "식모는 그런 고급은 먹엉 안 되는 거라" 하고 퉁명스럽게 거절하면서 자리를 피하곤 하는 것이었다.

또 하루 저녁은 늦은 저녁상을 혼자 받는데 삼촌이 상을 들여다 놓고 얼른 부엌으로 쫓아가더니 석쇠를 들고 왔다. 웬일인가 했더니 삼촌은 그 생선 껍질이 눌어붙은 석쇠를 보이면서 밥상에 오른 구운 생선이 부스러진 이유

From that day on, I was determined to take major corrective actions about my prejudice against my hometown, which, up to that point, had manifested itself simply as a vague sort of evasion. Undoubtedly it was Samch'on's presence that kept me mindful of my birthplace. Now I began to speak in my native dialect that I hadn't had a chance to use during my fifteen years in Seoul. It was mostly with Samch'on that I used my native tongue, but I also managed to pass quite a few idioms on to little Min-gi. In fact, I had been dismayed watching my boy growing up to be a meticulous and calculating Seoulite just like his tidy, fair-skinned mother. Whether he took after her or just watched too much TV, his eyesight was already so poor that he needed glasses at the age of five. While my wife was planning to have him take piano lessons, I was hoping to teach him to speak the robust vernacular of my hometown. It would be unacceptable to me if my son, too, rejected his father's birthplace even as I did. No doubt. How pretentious and perverted it had been for me to only speak the standard Seoul dialect all these years. I had led nothing short of a plagiarized, inauthentic life.

Yet, rarely, if ever, did we find Sun-i Samch'on in

를 해명하는 것이 아닌가. 생선이 석쇠에 들러붙어서 부서진 것이지 당신이 입질해서 그 모양이 된 게 아니라는 것이었다. 나는 하도 어이가 없어서 말이 안 나왔다. 왜 생선이 부서졌느냐고 누가 묻기라도 했단 말인가. 왜 묻지도 않았는데 그런 자격지심이 생겼을까? 당신의 결벽증은 정말 지독한 것이었다.

결국 나는 완전히 손들고 말았다. 오해를 풀어 드리려고 얼마나 진력을 다했던가. 그러나 순이삼촌은 완강한 패각의 껍데기를 뒤집어쓰고 꿈쩍도 않고 막무가내로 우리를 오해하는 것이었다. 그 오해는 증오와 같이 이글이글 타는 강렬한 감정이었다.

그동안 시골 딸에게서 편지가 두 번 온 모양인데 두 번 다 아내가 몰래 훔쳐보니까, 외손주가 할머니를 찾는다고 어서 내려오라는 내용이었다. 그래서 나는 순이삼촌이 곧 내려가리라고는 생각하고 있었지만 그새 오해가 풀리지 않아 무슨 원수처럼 헤어지게 되면 어쩌나 하고 걱정을 하게 되었다. 그러나 짐작과는 반대로 당신은 내려갈 의사를 전혀 비치지 않았다.

그러다가 시골서 사위가 올라왔다. 나보다 칠 년 연하인 사위 장씨는 농촌지도원으로 수원 농촌진흥원에 출장

a cheerful mood again, as her feelings were probably deeply injured by that incident. In fact, she hardly spoke. She seemed to harbor the kind of pain and anger our profuse apologies couldn't soothe. Eventually she clashed with my wife face-to-face.

One evening I came home late from work to find my wife and Samch'on arguing. Upon seeing me, Samch'on plopped down on the kitchen floor and started crying. I glared at my wife angrily and demanded to know what was going on. Now tears were streaming down my wife's cheeks. Damn it.

According to my wife, she had casually said, "We've already run out of rice?" in response when Samch'on had informed her that there was no more rice in the house and it was time to get some more. She insisted that her simple acknowledgment of this fact, equivalent to a careless nod, must have been misconstrued by Samch'on, perhaps because of her unfamiliarity with the nuances of the Seoulite manner of speaking, as a retort implying *How could it be gone so fast?* That would explain why Samch'on was wailing, "Do you mean it ran out sooner because I ate too much, or are you suggesting I stole it like a thief to sell in the market?" I was flabbergasted. The

온 것이었다. 아니, 장모를 모셔 갈 작정으로 남의 출장을 가로채가지고 올라왔다고 했다. 의지할 데라곤 딸자식 하나밖에 없는 노인을 어떻게 객지 생활을 하도록 놔두겠느냐는 것이었다. 무엇보다 남부끄러워 못 견디겠다고 했다. 삼촌은 서울 올라올 때, 혹시 못 가게 막을까 봐 딸네 집에 알리지 않고 몰래 올라왔던 모양이었다.

그러나 사위가 찾아와 같이 내려가재도 순이삼촌은 웬일인지 싫다고 고집을 세웠다. 애초에 마음먹은 대로 남의 집살이 일 년을 다 채우고 내려가겠노라고 했다. 우리 내외와 원만치 못하게 지내 온 푼수로 봐서는 미련 없이 훌훌 떠나 버릴 것 같은 분이 그냥 눌러 있겠다니 우리로선 참 고마운 생각이 들었다. 사람 구하기 어려운 때라 아쉬운 생각에서가 아니라, 우리를 그토록 오해했으면서도 딱 잘라 매정하게 돌아서 버리지 않는 그 마음씀이 더없이 고맙게 여겨졌다. 아마 순이삼촌 자신도 시간을 두고 오해를 풀고 가야지 하고 생각하고 있을지 모를 일이었다.

그런데 모든 것은 사위 장씨의 입에서 밝혀졌다.

그날 밤 장씨는 내 권유에 못 이겨 우리 집에서 자고 갔는데, 내가 삼촌이 우리를 오해하게 된 여러 사례를 들려주자 그는 그럴 줄 알았다고 하며, 아무래도 장모를 두고

absurdity of the situation left me at my wits' end not knowing how to resolve it or even where to start. Watching Samch'on heartbroken, caught in a trap over such a trivial matter, I was reduced to tears.

I remember how hard my wife and I tried that day to relieve Samch'on of her misapprehension. However, our efforts proved to be utterly futile as she began to show strange fastidiousness from then on. As if she had concluded that she had used more rice than necessary by making it too soft, thereby producing more crust, she seemed to strain her nerves trying to cook drier rice, a relentless obsession that weighed heavily upon her. I didn't dare complain though I much prefer tender, moist rice due to my weak digestion from low stomach acid. Worse yet, it was beyond heartbreaking and almost chilling to find her measuring rice all day long less than ten days after we got a new supply, trying to gauge how much had been consumed.

After these two similar episodes, my wife watched her own words and actions almost to a fault in order to avoid any possible misunderstanding by Sun-i Samch'on. It was evident to me that there had been a striking change in the way she dealt with Samch'on. The sullen rigidity of Samch'on's face

가는 것이 걱정이라고 했다. 그의 속삭이는 말로는 순이 삼촌은 심한 신경쇠약 환자라는 것이었다. 게다가 환청 증세까지 있어 시골에 있을 때도, 한 적이 없는 말을 들었노라고, 보지도 않은 흉을 봤다고 따지고 들기를 잘했다는 것이었다. 그러니 '밥 많이 먹는 식모'라는 것도, 우리에게 품은 오해도 모두 환청 때문에 생긴 것이 틀림없다고 말했다. 역시 그랬었구나. 옆에서 얘기를 듣던 아내는 방정맞게 안도의 한숨까지 내쉬었다. 당신의 신경쇠약은 지독한 결벽증과도 서로 얽혀진 것인데 이런 증세는 꽤나 해묵은 것이라고 했다. 그건 사오 년 전 콩 두 말을 훔쳤다는 억울한 누명을 썼을 때 얻은 병이었다. 하루는 이웃집에서 길에 멍석을 펴고 내다 넌 메주콩 두 말이 감쪽같이 없어졌는데 그 혐의를 평소에 사이가 안 좋던 순이삼촌에게 씌워 놓았다. 두 집은 서로 했느니 안 했느니 하면서 옥신각신 다투다가 그 집 여편네가 파출소에 가서 따지자고 당신의 팔을 잡아끌었던 모양인데 파출소 가자는 말에 당신은 대번에 기가 죽으면서 거기는 못 간다고 주저앉아 버리더라는 것이었다. 그러니 자연히 당신이 콩을 훔친 것으로 소문나 버릴밖에. 당신이 그전서부터 파출소를 피해 다니는 이상한 기피증이 있다는 걸 아는 사람은

never softened, however. She was unmistakably keeping away even from me. She insisted on paying for a few pictures of her I had taken during an outing at a park. Asked to join us for a glass of tomato juice, she would decline with a blunt comment such as "It's too luxurious for a kitchen maid" and disappear.

I was sitting down to a late supper by myself one evening when Samch'on hurried back to the kitchen after serving the food and returned with a handheld gridiron. Holding up the gridiron with some fish skin still stuck on it, she explained to me—I was befuddled—that the grilled fish on the plate was in pieces because it fell apart on the grid, not because she had sampled some of it. I was absolutely speechless with disbelief. Did anyone ever ask her why the fish was in tatters? Where on earth did her guilty conscience come from? Her obsessiveness was truly extreme.

In the end, I threw up my hands. I had done my very best to dispel her misconceptions. Regardless, Sun-i Samch'on turned a deaf ear and adamantly clung to her misreading of our intentions, while stubbornly holed up inside a thick shell of resistance. Her misunderstanding was an all-powerful,

알고 있었지만 그건 일단 씌워진 누명을 벗기는 데 별 도움이 되지 않았다. 당신은 1949년에 있었던 마을 소각 때 깊은 정신적 상처를 입어, 불에 놀란 사람 부지깽이만 봐도 놀란다는 격으로 군인이나 순경을 먼빛으로만 봐도 질겁하고 지레 피하던 신경 증세가 진작부터 있어 온 터였다. 하여간 당신은 그 콩 두 말 사건으로 심한 정신적 충격을 입었던 모양으로 절간에서 두어 달 정양까지 해야 했다. 그때부터 당신은 심한 결벽증에 사로잡혀 혹시 누가 뒤에서 흉보지 않나 하는 생각에 붙잡혀 늘 전전긍긍하게 되고, 나중엔 환청 증세까지 겹쳐 하지 않은 말을 들었노라고 따지고 들곤 했다. 그리고 서울 우리 집에 올라올 무렵에는, 상군 해녀이던 당신이 갑자기 물이 무서워져서 물질마저 그만두었다는 것이었다.

순이삼촌은 사위를 홀로 내려 보낸 뒤 우리 집에서 석 달 가까이 더 지냈다. 그러나 우리의 기대와는 달리 당신은 오해를 풀어 주기는커녕 오히려 새로운 오해를 자꾸 만들어 보태 가는 것이었다. 그러다가 당신은 끝내 일 년을 다 못 채우고 고향에 내려온 것인데 내려온 지 한 달도 못되어 이 일이 발생했으니, 나로서는 일말의 가책을 안 느낄 도리가 없었다. 아니, 양심의 가책이라니, 내가 무슨

burning emotion, akin to hatred.

During that period, she had received two letters from her daughter at home, both of which my wife managed to read unbeknownst to Samch'on. In both cases, the daughter implored Samch'on to come home on the pretext that her granddaughter was asking for Grandma. While naturally expecting Sun-i Samch'on to go back before long, I was also troubled about parting with her seemingly on antagonistic terms without resolving any issues first. Contrary to our assumption, however, she betrayed no intention to go back home.

It was around then that her son-in-law came to Seoul from down south. Seven years younger than I, Mr. Chang, who works at the local office of the Agricultural Development Agency, was on a business trip to the agency's headquarters in Suwŏn. In fact, he said, he had taken over someone else's trip just so he could escort his mother-in-law back home. How could they let an elderly woman live in an unfamiliar place far from home, when her sole source of support was her one and only daughter? he asked. He said he couldn't bear the shame any longer. Apparently, Samch'on came to Seoul without telling her daughter and her family, fearing they

잘못이 있나. 나도 골치를 썩이며 당신에게 꽤 하노라고 하지 않았던가. 당신은 한마디로 불가항력이었다. 그럼에도 결과론으로 따져 순이삼촌의 서울 생활이 여의치 못했으리라고 짐작하고 있을 친척 어른들을 마주 대하기가 참으로 면구스러웠다.

나는 이런저런 생각으로 머리가 지끈지끈 아파 바람벽에 머리를 기대고 눈을 감았다. 그래도 시원찮아 염치 불고하고 길수 형 등 뒤로 가 바람벽을 마주보고 잠깐 누웠다. 문풍지를 푸르르 떨게 하며 창틈으로 들어오는 찬바람이 지끈거리는 이마를 식혀 주었다. 바람은 또 때때로 강하게 불어와 싸락눈을 창호지창에 훅훅 뿌려 놓곤 했다. 그건 고양이가 앞발로 창을 긁어대는 소리처럼 을씨년스럽게 들렸다. 왜 고향엔 유별나게 싸락눈이 많을까? 바람 많이 부는 기상 때문일까? 아니다. 그건 언제나 고구마, 조팝을 상식하는 고향 사람들에게 내리는 산디쌀일 것이다. 모처럼 제삿날에나 먹어 보던 '곤밥'. 왜 '곤밥'이라고 했을까? '곤밥'은 '고운밥'에서 왔을 것이고 쌀밥은 빛깔이 고우니까. 어린 시절에도 파제 후 '곤밥'을 몇 숟갈 얻어먹어 보려고 길수 형과 나는 어른들 등 뒤에서 이렇게 모로 누워 새우잠을 자곤 했다. 제상마저 소각 때 태워

would object.

Samch'on stood firm for some unknown reason, even though her son-in-law had traveled this distance to plead with her to return home with him. She insisted that she fulfill her original plan to serve as our domestic help for a year. My wife and I were deeply grateful for her decision to stay, because, given all the stress and strain between us up to that point, we were prepared to see her leaving without hesitation. It wasn't that we were afraid we'd have a tough time replacing her but that we truly appreciated her kindness in deciding against coldly turning her back on us in spite of the serious misgivings she had about us. Maybe Samch'on, too, was thinking that she should take the time and make the effort to resolve her issues with us before leaving.

It turned out that her son-in-law, Mr. Chang, had all the answers to our questions.

That night I successfully begged him to stay overnight with us. I had a chance to tell him about the several situations through which Samch'on had come to misunderstand us. He said he had expected as much and wasn't comfortable leaving his mother-in-law with us. He lowered his voice to add that Sun-i Samch'on had a severe nervous breakdown.

먹고 송진내 물씬 나는 날송판때기 위에다 제물이라곤 마른 생선 하나에 메밀묵 한 쟁반, 고사리, 무채 각각 한 보시기밖에 진설할 것이 없던 그 어려운 시절이었지만, 메는 꼭 산디쌀밥이었다. 자정이 넘어 큰아버지가 우리들을 깨워 세수하고 오라고 방 밖으로 떠밀었을 때 마당에 하얗게 깔려 있던 것도 싸락눈이었다. 그 시간이면 이 집 저 집에서 그 청승맞은 곡성이 터지고 거기에 맞춰 개 짖는 소리가 밤하늘로 치솟아 오르곤 했다. 한날한시에 이 집 저 집 제사가 시작되는 것이었다. 이날 우리 집 할아버지 제사는 고모의 울음소리부터 시작되곤 했다. 이어 큰어머니가 부엌일을 보다 말고 나와 울음을 터뜨리면 당숙모가 그 뒤를 따랐다. 아, 한날한시에 이 집 저 집에서 터져 나오던 곡소리, 음력 섣달 열여드렛날, 낮에는 이곳저곳에서 추렴 돼지가 먹구슬나무에 목매달려 죽는 소리에 온 마을이 시끌짝했고 오백 위도 넘는 귀신들이 밥 먹으러 강신하는 한밤중이면 슬픈 곡성이 터졌다. 그러나 철부지 우리 어린것들은 이 골목 저 골목 흔해진 죽은 돼지 오줌통을 가져다가 오줌 지린내를 참으며 보릿짚대로 바람을 탱탱하게 불어넣어 축구공 삼아 신나게 차고 놀곤 했다. 우리는 한밤중의 그 지긋지긋한 곡소리가 딱 질색이었다.

More than once in the past back home she even showed symptoms of auditory hallucinations, where she would start arguing with others over some comments or criticisms that were apparently never made but that she insisted she had overheard. He was quite convinced that the "famished kitchen maid" gossip and all her misapprehensions about us could be attributed to these hallucinations. So it was as I suspected. After listening in, my wife even breathed a presumptuous sigh of relief. According to Mr. Chang, Samch'on's nervous breakdown, which was inseparable from her extreme fastidiousness, was a longstanding condition.

Her breakdown had been triggered about four or five years earlier when she was unfairly accused of having stolen a large quantity of soybeans. One day, one of her neighbors spread a few bags of beans out to dry on a straw mat by the roadside, only to discover later that they had disappeared without a trace. The neighbor, who was not exactly on friendly terms with Samch'on, pinned the blame on her. At some point while the two were squabbling over Samch'on's culpability, the neighbor apparently pulled Samch'on by the arm, challenging her to take the matter to the police. At the mention

자정 넘어 제사 시간을 기다리며 듣던 소각 당시의 그 비참한 이야기도 싫었다. 하도 들어서 귀에 못이 박힌 이야기. 왜 어른들은 아직 아이인 우리에게 그런 끔찍한 이야기를 되풀이해서 들려주었을까?

그리고 파제 후 이 집 저 집 지붕 위에 던져 올린 퇴줏그릇의 세 숟갈 밥을 먹으러 날 새자마자 날아드는 까마귀들도 기분 나빴다. 까마귀가 죽은 귀신의 혼령이라든가, 저승차사라고 하는 것 때문이 아니라, 그 광택 있는 검은 날개빛이 마을 어른들을 잡으러 오던 서청 순경들의 옷빛하고 너무 흡사했기 때문이었다. 사람을 얕보던 까마귀들. 사람이 다가가도, 우여우여 소리쳐도 달아날 줄 몰랐다. 그것들은 시체가 널린 보리밭을 까맣게 뒤덮고 파먹다가 심심하면 겨울 하늘로 떼 지어 날아오르며 세찬 날갯짓으로 하늬바람 타기를 잘했다. 그 당시 일주 도로변에 있는 순이삼촌네 밭처럼 옴팡진 밭 다섯 개에는 죽은 시체들이 허옇게 널려 있었다. 밭담에도, 지붕에도, 듬북눌에도, 먹구슬나무에도 어디에나 앉아 있던 까마귀들. 까마귀들만이 시체를 파먹은 게 아니었다. 마을 개들도 시체를 뜯어먹고 다리 토막을 입에 물고 다녔다. 사람 시체를 파먹어 미쳐 버린 이 개들은 나중에 경찰 총에 맞아

of the police, Samch'on suddenly seemed to have lost all her spirit and simply plopped down on the ground, flatly refusing to go to the police station. Quite predictably, the ensuing gossip branded her as a bean thief. Some people were well aware that Samch'on had already clearly exhibited an unusual phobia about police stations, which made it all the more difficult for her to be cleared of the allegation of theft already leveled against her. Since Samch'on suffered severe psychological trauma in 1949 when the village was torched, the mere sight of a soldier or police officer from a distance would frighten her enough to make her take a long detour, and this symptom of her nervous breakdown was well known to some of the locals. As the old saying goes, someone burnt by fire tends to jump at the sight of a poker. At any rate, distress over the missing soybeans was evidently damaging enough to send her to a Buddhist temple for a few months of respite. Samch'on had been a victim of acute phobia ever since, constantly obsessing over whether someone was badmouthing her. Later on, her obsessive compulsive behavior was compounded by auditory hallucinations, which often led her to falsely accuse others of making the remarks she insisted she had

죽었지만, 그 많던 까마귀들은 모두 어디 갔을까? 아까 낮에 까마귀가 눈에 안 띄기에 길수 형에게 물어보았지만 그도 고개를 갸우뚱할 뿐이었다. 농작물에 큰 피해가 될 정도로 그렇게 번성하던 까마귀들이 사오 년 전부터는 웬일인지 별로 보이지 않는다는 것이었다.

문득 큰당숙어른의 감기 쉰 목소리가 들려왔다. 나는 뉘었던 몸을 일으키고 바로 앉았다.

"순이아지망은 죽어도 발쎄 죽을 사람이여. 밭을 에워 싸고 베락같이 총질해댔는디 그 아지망만 살 한 점 안 상하고 살아났으니 참 신통한 일이랐쥬."

"아매도 사격 직전에 기절해연 쓰러진 모양입니다. 깨난 보니 자기 우에 죽은 사람이 여럿이 포개져 덮연 있었댄 허는 걸 보민…… 그때 발쎄 그 아지망은 정신이 어긋나 버린 거라 마씸" 하고 작은당숙어른이 말을 받았다.

"해필 그 밭이 순이아지망네 밭이었으니."

"그 밭이서 죽은 사름들이 몽창몽창 썩어 거름되연 이듬해엔 감저(고구마) 농사는 참 잘되어서. 감저가 목침덩어리만씩 큼직큼직해시니까."

"그핸 숭년이라, 보릿겨범벅 먹던 때랐지만 그 아지망네 밭에서 난 감저는 사름 죽은 밭엣 거라고 사름들이 사

heard. By the time she came to Seoul, this first-rate veteran diver had also given up on diving altogether from a sudden fear of water.

Sun-i Samch'on stayed with us for three more months after turning her son-in-law away. To our dismay, instead of letting go of her previous suspicions, she acquired some new ones. In the end, she went home without completing her one-year commitment. Since her death took place less than a month after her return, I couldn't help feeling guilty to some extent. Wait a minute. Why guilt? What did I do wrong? Didn't I agonize sufficiently over her welfare? To be blunt, she was impossible. Nonetheless, I was absolutely mortified to be faced with the elders of the clan who must be suspecting, quite rightly, that Sun-i Samch'on's stay in Seoul wasn't exactly a picnic.

I had a pounding headache from these tangled thoughts, so I rested my head against the wall and closed my eyes. Not getting sufficient relief, I lay down behind Cousin Kil-su for a break, even in the presence of the elders. The cold air, wafting through the cracks around the window frame and vibrating the fringe of the window-paper, cooled my overheated forehead. From time to time, gusts

먹질 안 했쥬."

"그 아지망이 필경엔 바로 그 밭이서 죽고 말아시니, 쯧쯧."

어른들의 이런 이야기를 들으며 나는 야릇한 착각에 사로잡혔다. 순이삼촌은 한 달 보름 전에 죽은 게 아니라 이미 삼십 년 전 그날 그 밭에서 죽은 게 아닐까 하고.

이렇게 순이삼촌이 단서가 되어 이야기는 시작되었다. 그 흉물스럽던 까마귀들도 사라져 버리고, 세월이 삼십 년이니 이제 괴로운 기억을 잊고 지낼 만도 하건만 고향 어른들은 그렇지가 않았다. 오히려 잊힐까 봐 제삿날마다 모여 이렇게 이야기를 하며 그때 일을 명심해 두는 것이었다.

어린 시절 제사 때마다 귀에 못이 박힐 정도로 들었던 그 이야기들이 다시 머릿속에 무성하게 피어올랐다.

그 사건은 당시 일곱 살 나이던 내게도 큰 충격을 주었다. 사건 바로 전해에 폐병으로 시름시름 앓던 어머니가 돌아가시고 도피자라는 낙인을 받고 노상 마룻장 밑에 숨어 살던 아버지마저 일본으로 밀항해 가 버려 졸지에 고아가 되어 버린 나는 큰집에 얹혀살고 있었다. 죽은 어머니 생각에 걸핏하면 남몰래 눈물짓던 내가 그 울음을 졸

of wind tossed small pellets of dry snow with a whoosh against the window, making a desolate sound, as if a cat were scratching at the paper. Why is there so much dry snow in my hometown? Because of the windy climate? No. It must be "dry-land rice" falling from above for village folks, who live mostly on potatoes and millet. *Kon* rice was served only after memorial services. Where did the name *kon* rice come from? It must have originated from *koun*, a word that means 'beautiful,' since cooked white *kon* rice has a beautiful hue.

Growing up, Cousin Kil-su and I would fall asleep curled up between the elders and the wall while waiting for the ceremony to end so we could be treated to a few spoonfuls of *kon* rice. Without fail, cooked dry-land rice was offered on the altar even in that destitute time when all we could afford as offerings were a plate of dried fish, a tray of buck-wheat curd, and a bowl each of wild fern and shredded radish, served up on an unfinished pine wood panel that still smelled strongly of fresh sap, since even the tables for memorial ceremonies had been torched during the Scorched Earth Operation. When Uncle woke us up right after midnight and nudged us outside to wash up in preparation for the

업한 것은 음력 선달 열여드렛날의 그 사건이 내 어린 가슴팍을 짓밟고 지나간 뒤였다. 말하자면 너무 놀란 나머지 울음이 뚝 떨어진 거였다. 그리고 일주 도로변 옴팡진 밭마다 흔전만전 허옇게 널려 있던 시체를 직접 내 눈으로 보고 나자 나는 어머니의 죽음이 유독 나에게만 닥쳐온 불행이 아니고 그 숱한 죽음 중의 하나일 뿐이라고 생각되었다. 사실 어머니가 폐병으로 죽지 않고 살아 있었다 하더라도 그날 그 사건에 말려 어차피 죽고 말았을 것이다.

"그날 헛간에 앉안 멕(멱서리)을 잣고 있는디 군인들이 완(와서) 연설 들으레 오랜 하지 안 해여." 큰당숙어른이 먼저 말을 꺼냈다.

음력 선달 열여드렛날, 그날은 유달리 바람 끝이 맵고 시린 날씨였다. 그래서 여편네들은 돈지코지 미역밭에 나가 물질할 엄두를 못 내고 집에서 물레로 양말 짤 실을 잣거나, 텃밭의 배추 포기에 오줌 거름을 주든지, 시아버지를 도와 지붕 이엉이 바람에 날아가지 않게 동여맬 동아줄을 띠풀로 꼬고 있었다. 그 무렵 젊은축들은 공연히 도피자로 몰려 낮에는 마을에서 사오리 한라산 쪽으로 올라간 큰 냇가 자연 동굴에 숨어 있다가 밤에나 내려오는 박

ceremony, we found dry snow blanketing the yard. Around that time, the depressing wails of mourning would break out from every other house, followed by the howls of dogs, piercing the night sky. Memorial ceremonies were beginning in so many households at the same time.

In our household, the memorial service for our grandfather usually started with Paternal Aunt's wails of bereavement. Soon, Uncle's wife would drop whatever she was doing in the kitchen to come out and join her, followed by my *tangsuk*'s wife. Oh, the cries of grieving that erupted from so many houses simultaneously on the 18th of December. During the day, the entire village was filled with the final squeals of sacrificial pigs paid for with funds raised by multiple households and hung from black pearl trees around the village. At midnight, when over five hundred spirits descended for the offerings, heart-wrenching cries erupted everywhere. Even so, clueless children like us would pick up the pig bladders scattered abundantly in alleyways, and enduring the stench of urine, use barley straws to inflate them until they were hard. Then we had a great time kicking them around like soccer balls to our hearts' content.

쥐 생활을 계속하고 있었다.

그날 아침나절에 길수 형과 나는 큰아버지를 도와 밭거름으로 쓰려고 밤사이 갯가에 올라온 뜸부기나 감태 따위 해초를 한군데 모아 놓는 일을 했다. 그러고는 집에 돌아와서 점심 요기로 할머니가 내준 식은 고구마 한 자루씩 받아먹고 있노라니까 별안간 밖에서 호루라기 소리가 요란하고 고함 소리가 들렸다.

"연설 들으러 나오시오! 한 사람도 빠짐없이 국민학교 운동장으로 모이시오!"

보통 때 같으면 순경이나 대동청년단원 몇 사람이 다니면서 사람들을 불러 모았는데 이번엔 어쩐 일인지 철모에 총까지 든 군인들이 수십 명 퍼져 다니면서 득달같이 재촉하는 것이 뭔가 심상치 않았다. 심지어는 총검으로 창문을 열어젖히면서 병든 노인까지 내몰았다. 좀 불안한 생각이 없지도 않았지만, 그 전해 5·10 선거 무렵에도 그렇게 득달같이 사람들을 불러 모은 적이 있어서 그때처럼 무슨 중요한 연설이 있는가 보다라고만 생각했다.

길수 형과 나는 할머니와 큰아버지 뒤를 따라 국민학교로 갔다. 먼저 온 동네 아이들 여남은 명이 벌써 조회대 밑에 진을 치고 있었다. 시국 강연회는 아이들에게 퍽 인

We absolutely loathed the wearisome midnight wailing. Nor were we particularly fond of those stories of misery from the time of the Scorched Earth Operation that we heard while waiting for the ceremony to begin. Those tired old tales were drummed into our heads. Why did the elders repeat such horrifying stories to us when we were little kids?

Just as ominous were the swarms of crows that would flock at the crack of dawn for the three spoonfuls of cooked rice tossed from wine bowls up onto the roofs of houses after the ceremony. Not that we believed the crows were actually the spirits of the dead or messengers from the netherworld, but the shiny black of their wings reminded us of the tint of the uniforms worn by the Northwestern Youth Corps police who came to arrest the villagers. The crows weren't afraid of people. They wouldn't budge even when humans approached them and yelled at them to shoo. They covered the body-strewn barley fields like black blankets and gorged themselves before flying off in swarms into the winter sky, as if weary and in need of a break, skillfully riding the west wind with the forceful beating of their wings. At that time, the five sunken patches of field, including Sun-i Samch'on's, abutting the loop

기가 있었다. 그 당시 연사들에게 유행하던 신파조의 웅변이 퍽 재미있고 맨 끝 순서로 부르는 〈역적의 남로당을 때려 부숴라〉라는 씩씩한 노래와 우렁찬 만세 삼창은 정말 가슴 뛰게 하는 것이었다. 길수 형과 나는 할머니 곁을 떠나 아이들 있는 데로 가 쪼그리고 앉았다. 운동장 흙은 진눈깨비가 녹은 다음이라 몹시 질척거렸는데 밑창 터진 고무신에 물이 새어 들었다. 나는 발이 젖어 시렸지만 참고 기다렸다.

"그때 운동장에 뫼인 사람 수가 대강 얼매나 되어시까마씸?" 하고 육촌 현모 형이 물었다. 형은 당시 열댓 살 나이에 도피자로 몰려 피해 다녔으므로 요행히 그날 사건 현장에는 없었다.

"겔쎄, 마을 호수가 삼백 호가 넘어시니까 한 천 명쯤 안 됐이까? 병든 할망들까장 부축해연 나와시니까" 하고 큰당숙어른이 말하자 큰아버지가 참견했다.

"아니 그보다 많을 거여, 선흘리와 논흘리 쪽에서 소개해연 온 사람들도 건줌(거의) 백 명은 되어시니까."

잠시 후 돌과 흙으로 쌓아 올린 조회대 위로 권총 찬 장교가 올라섰다. 그 장교의 지시에 따라 모두 질척거리는 땅에 쪼그리고 앉았다. 강연이 시작되나 보다 했는데 웬

road were white with scattered bodies. On the stone walls dividing the patches, on the roofs, on the piles of seaweed, in the black pearl trees—everywhere we turned, there were crows. Crows weren't the only creatures feeding on human bodies. Village dogs would also bite off body parts and run around carrying chunks of human legs in their mouths. Those dogs that went mad from sinking their teeth into corpses were later shot to death by the police, but where did all the crows go? I asked Cousin Kil-su, after noticing their absence, and he wasn't sure. He acknowledged, however, that the crows, having multiplied to the point where they were a major threat to the crops, curiously had all but disappeared about four or five years ago.

Abruptly the voice of Older Tangsuk, hoarse from a common cold, interrupted my thoughts. I raised my torso off the floor and sat up straight.

"Ms. Sun-i enjoyed an extra lease on life. It was a wonder in the first place that she walked away without a scratch, the sole survivor of that thunderous barrage from all sides of that field."

"It seems that she fell to the ground unconscious right before the shooting began, given her own account that she woke up buried underneath layers

걸 장교는 지서 박 주임과 이장 강씨를 단 위로 불러 세우더니 지금부터 군인 가족을 골라내겠다고 큰 소리로 언명하지 않는가.

"군인 가족들은 앞으로 나오시오. 사돈에 팔촌까장 덮어 놓고 나오디 말구 직계가족만 나오라요. 만일 군인 직계가족도 아닌데 나온 사람은 당장 엄벌에 터하가시오."

단 밑에는 입산자 색출 때문에 종종 마을에 나타나던 함덕지서 순경 두 명과 창끝이 검게 그을린 대창을 든 대동청년단 청년 예닐곱 명이 뻣뻣한 자세로 서 있고 그 뒤로 스무 명쯤 되어 보이는 무장 군인들이 이열횡대로 늘어서 있었다. 그들의 한결같이 굳은 표정을 보자 사람들은 적이 불안을 느끼기 시작했다. 영문 모르는 그들은 옆 사람을 바라보며 수군거리고 주위를 둘러보았다. 별안간에 무슨 일일까? 군인 가족들에게 보리쌀 배급이라도 주려나? 막상 군인 가족 당사자들도 나가야 좋을지 몰라 우물쭈물하고 있자, 장교는 빨리 나오라고 빽 고함을 질렀다. 군인 가족들은 주뼛주뼛 눈치 보면서 앞으로 나갔다. 그들은 단 앞으로 가 이장과 순경과 대동청년단 사람들의 심사를 받고 나서 단 뒤로 인솔되어 따로 앉혀졌다.

"아명해도(아무래도) 낌새가 이상해연 나도 어머님을 찾

of bodies.... Her mind had gone awry right then and there, I'd bet," Younger Tangsuk chimed in.

"It all happened in the field that belongs to none other than Ms. Sun-i herself."

"Those who died there decomposed into mushy fertilizer, which produced a bumper crop of potatoes and sweet potatoes the following year. Those potatoes were as big as wooden pillows."

"It was a year of poor yield where we had to live on barley bran porridge, but folks refused to buy or eat the potatoes from that woman's patch because of all the dead on her land."

"In the end, she wound up dying in the very same field, *tsk tsk*."

Listening to these accounts by the elders, I had the strange illusion that Sun-i Samch'on had died in that field not a month and a half ago but thirty years before.

So began the storytelling occasioned by Sun-i Samch'ons fate. Now that the hideous crows had disappeared and thirty years had passed, the elders of my hometown could have been free of their painful memories. But they didn't seem to be. To the contrary, they gathered together every memorial day and shared their stories to re-inscribe the events of

안 뵈시고 군인 가족들 틈에 섞연 나갔쥬. 매부가 군인이니 직계가족은 아니지만 다행히 이장 강씨가 눈감아 주언 넘어갔쥬." 큰아버지의 말이었다.

"형님 그것 봅서. 누이동생을 나한치 팔아 무신 손핼 봅디까? 이북것한티 시집간다고 결사반대허더니" 하고 고무부가 너털웃음을 웃었다.

그다음에 순경 가족이 나가고 이어서 공무원 가족이 나갈 즈음 뭔가 좋지 않은 낌새를 눈치챈 군중은 동요하기 시작했다. 공무원 가족에 이어 마지막으로 대동청년단과 국민회 간부 차례가 왔을 때 사람들은 너도나도 앞을 다투어 나아가 이장과 청년단 사람들에게 매달렸다.

"정숙이 아버지, 우리 친정 오래비가 작년에 병정 간 거 무사(왜) 알지 않우꽈?"

"이장님 마씸, 우리 사촌 동상이 금녕지서에 순경으로 있우다. 김갑재라고 마씸."

"뒤로 물러갑서. 다들 직계가족이 아니라 아니됩니다. 물러갑서."

이장은 손을 내저었다.

"직계가족이 뭐우꽈?"

"이장님. 날 좀 내보내 줍서."

that day in their own memories so as to never forget.

Stories that had been told and retold at every memorial service—to the point of forming a callus on our young ears—mushroomed luxuriantly in my mind once again.

The event had an enormous impact on me as a seven-year-old, as well. The year before, my mother had passed away after a drawn-out battle with tuberculosis and my father had stowed away to Japan, effectively ending his extended exile, branded as an escapee, in a hideaway under the floor of our house. Suddenly orphaned, I was living with my uncle's family on their largesse. It was after the event of December 18 trampled my tender heart that I grew out of the habit of crying in private for my dead mother. The overwhelming shock stopped me cold from crying, in other words. What's more, witnessing firsthand all those casually scattered bodies whitening every sunken patch of field along the loop road, I realized I wasn't the only one who had the misfortune of losing a mother, that my mother's death was merely one of many. Indeed, even if she had survived her illness, she wouldn't have survived the events of that day.

이런 북새통에 별안간 군중 속에서 날카로운 부르짖음 소리가 났다.

"불났져! 마을에 불났져!"

화들짝 놀란 사람들이 우르르 몰려가 학교 돌담 울타리에 기어올랐다.

"불이여, 불", "불났져, 불났져", "아이고, 아이고." 운동장 사방에서 울부짖는 소리가 회오리바람처럼 일어나 하늘을 찔렀다. 울타리까지 갈 것 없이 마을 동편 하늘에 까맣게 불티가 날고 있는 게 내 눈에도 역력히 보였다. 매캐한 연기 냄새도 차츰 바람에 밀려왔다. 그때 서편 울타리 돌담이 여기저기서 매달린 사람들의 체중에 못 이겨 와르르 무너졌다. 사람들이 그 울타리 터진 데로 몰려 밖으로 나가려고 하자 지체 없이 총소리가 울렸다. 사람들은 다시 운동장 복판으로 우르르 몰려들었다. 무너진 돌담 위에 흰 무명적삼에 갈중의를 입은 노인이 한 사람 엎어져 죽은 모양인지 꼼짝하지 않았다. 군인 여남은 명이 빠른 동작으로 돌담 위로 뛰어오르더니 아래를 향해 총을 겨누었다. 그러자 조회대 뒤에 늘어서 있던 이십여 명의 군인들도 앞에총 자세로 잽싸게 뛰어나오더니 정면에서 사람들을 포위했다. 단상의 그 장교는 권총을 어깨 위로 빼들

Older Tangsuk broached the subject again: "I was weaving straw bags in the shed that day when soldiers arrived and told me to come hear a public speech."

On that 18th of December by the lunar calendar, the wind was unusually sharp and cold. Thus the women didn't dare to go diving in the kelp farm near Cape Tonji and instead stayed home spinning yarn for socks or fertilizing cabbages in the yard with urine or helping their fathers-in-law twisting tape grass into ropes with which to tie down thatched roofs to resist the wind. Around that time, most of the young men, unfairly branded fugitives, were living like bats, hiding during the day in the natural caves that lined the big stream half an hour's walk toward Mt. Halla, and coming down into the village only at night.

Cousin Kil-su and I had worked side by side all morning that day, helping Uncle gather a pile of seaweed, *tŭmbugi* and *kamt'ae* that had washed up overnight, to use as fertilizer. We had just come home and sat down to the cool steamed sweet potatoes Grandma prepared for lunch when we heard loud whistles and shouts outside.

"Come out for a speech! Everyone meet at the ele-

고 으름장을 놓았다. 그가 강하게 턱을 올려 젖히자 철모가 햇빛에 번쩍 빛났다

"잘 들으라요. 우리레 지금 작전 수행 등에 있소. 여러분의 집은 작전 명령에 따라 소각되는 거이오. 우리의 다음 임무는 여러분을 모두 제주읍으로 소개하는 거니끼니 소개둥 만약 질서를 안 지키는 자가 있으문 아까와 같이 가차 없이 총살할 거이니 명심하라우요."

장교의 귀 설은 이북 사투리가 겁 집어먹는 부락민들의 머리 위에 카랑카랑 울려 퍼졌다. 사람들은 제주읍으로 소개시킨다는 말에 반신반의하면서 군인들의 눈치를 살폈다. 지금 당장은 자기 집이 불타고 있다는 생각에만 완전히 넋 잃고 절망해야 할 사람들이 다른 무엇을 예감하고 두려워하는가? 마을 쪽에서 해풍을 타고 매캐한 연기 냄새가 더욱 심하게 밀려오고 불티가 까맣게 뜬 하늘에 불아지랑이가 어른거렸다. 게다가 이따금 총소리가 탕탕 울렸다.

"난 그날 섯동네에 쇠(소) 홍정하레 갔다 오던 참이랐우다. 마악 빌레동산 잔솔밭에 당도해연 내려다보난 묵은 구장네 집허구 종주네 집이 불붙어 있십디다. 잔솔밭이 숨어서 보난 군인들이 조짚뭇을 빼어다 불붙여 들고 이

mentary school yard, no exceptions!"

Usually police officers or a small group of United Youth Corps members would go around telling people to gather. But there was something out of the ordinary this time as dozens of soldiers, wearing helmets and even carrying guns, fanned out and relentlessly rounded up the villagers. They even busted windows open with their bayonets to drive out the elderly who were sick in bed. Though not entirely without misgivings, we assumed it was a public announcement as important as the one around the May 10 general election of the previous year, when there was a similarly forceful round-up.

Cousin Kil-su and I followed Grandma and Uncle to the elementary school. A dozen or so village kids who had gotten there ahead of us were already lined up right under the podium. Public lectures about current affairs were quite popular among kids. Not only did they find the melodramatic tone then in style quite entertaining, but the valiant song "Smash the Treasonous Southern Labor Party" and the thunderous three cheers that concluded such events always thrilled our hearts like nothing else. Cousin Kil-su and I left Grandma and squatted down next to the other kids. The schoolyard dirt, in

집 저 집 옮겨 댕기멍 추녀 끝뎅이에다 불을 당기고 이십디다."

군인들의 지시에 따라 사람들이 교문을 향해 늘어서기 시작했을 때, 별안간 "군인들이 우리를 죽이레 데려감져" 하는 말이 전류처럼 군중 속을 꿰뚫었다. 그러자 교문 가까이 선두에 섰던 사람들이 흩어지며 뒤로 우르르 몰려갔다. 단상의 장교가 권총을 휘두르며 뒤로 물러가는 자는 가차 없이 총살하겠다고 고래고래 소리 질렀다. 이 말에 사람들은 잠시 주춤했을 뿐 다시 뒷걸음치기 시작했다.

그때 큰아버지가 길게 한숨을 내쉬며 말했다.

"하이고, 난 그때 저 길수 놈하고 상수 녀석(나)을 얼마나 찾았는지 모를로고. 어머님하고 아명(아무리) 큰 소리로 불러도 이놈우 새끼들이 어디 가 박혀신지……."

할머니와 큰아버지가 번갈아 악쓰며 부르는 소리를 우리는 듣고 있었지만 갈팡질팡하는 사람들 틈에 섞여서 도무지 헤어나갈 수가 없었다. 우리는 둘 다 고무신이 벗겨진 채 사람들에게 이리 쏠리고 저리 쏠리면서 울고 있었다.

우리들은 서로 손을 꼭 붙잡고 놓지 않았다. 서로 이름 부르며 가족을 찾는 소리와 군인들의 악에 바친 욕 소리로 운동장은 온통 아수라장이었다.

which sleet had just melted, was slushy, and moisture seeped into my rubber shoes through cracks in the soles. My feet were wet and freezing but I persevered and waited without complaining.

"Roughly how many people do you suppose gathered in the schoolyard?" asked Second Cousin Hyŏnmo. About sixteen years old at the time, he was luckily absent from the scene, hiding because he was marked as an escapee.

"Well, about a thousand since the village had over three hundred households, I'd guess? Even grandmas in poor health came out with assistance," said Older Tangsuk, before Older Uncle interjected.

"No, it must have been more than that. There were almost a hundred evacuees from the Sŏnhŭl Village and Nonhŭl Village areas, as well."

Soon an army officer armed with a pistol stepped up on the podium made of rocks and dirt. Following his orders, everyone squatted down on the muddy ground. Much to our surprise, instead of giving the expected speech, the officer called Mr. Pak, the Police Chief, and Mr. Kang, the Village Chief, up onto the podium and declared in a booming voice that they were about to separate out military families.

머리 위에서 한 발의 총성이 벼락같이 터진 것은 바로 그때였다. 사람들은 일제히 “아이고!” 소리를 지르며 서편 울타리 쪽으로 우르르 몰려가 붙었다. 운동장은 순식간에 물 끼얹은 듯 조용해졌다. 사람들이 몰려가고 난 빈자리에 한 여편네가 앞으로 엎어져 있고 옆에는 젖먹이 아이가 내팽개쳐져 있었다. 조용한 가운데 그 아기만 바락바락 악을 쓰며 울고 있었다.

“영배 각시 총 맞았저!” 누군가 이렇게 속삭였다.

흰 적삼에 번진 붉은 선혈이 역력했다.

“두 살 난 그 아기가 바로 방앳간 허는 장식이여, 후제 외할망이 키웠쥬. 이젠 결혼도 하고 씨 멸족할 뻔한 집이서 아들 둘까지 낳아시니 죽은 어멍 복을 입은 것일 거라, 아매도.” 작은당숙의 말이었다.

죽은 사람을 보자 나는 더럭 겁이 났다. 사람들이 뒤로 물러나 앞이 트였지만 길수 형과 나는 장교가 권총을 빼들고 서 있는 조회대 뒤로 달려갈 엄두가 도무지 나지 않았다. 저쪽으로 가다간 저 사람이 틀림없이 총을 쏠 테지. 우리는 어찌할 바를 모르고 발을 동동 구르기만 했다.

사람들이 서편 울타리에 붙어 나올 생각을 하지 않자 군인들은 긴 장대 두 개를 들고 나왔다. 그건 교무실 앞

"All military families must step forward. I don't mean everyone, such as in-laws or third cousins, but immediate family members only. Anyone who isn't an immediate family member who steps forward will be subject to instant and severe punishment."

Standing stiff right under the podium were two police officers from the Hamdŏk police substation, who often showed up at the village searching for escapees who had gone into hiding in the mountains, and half a dozen members of the United Youth Corps holding bamboo spears with charred black tips. Behind them were about twenty armed soldiers in a double line. The hardened looks on all of their faces began to make the villagers feel somewhat uneasy. Perplexed, they looked at each other and whispered circumspectly. What's going on, out of the blue? Are military families going to get extra barley rations? The military families themselves hesitated, unsure whether it was wise to step forward. The officer yelled that they must step forward immediately. They emerged with tentative and cautious steps. They went up to the podium for screening by the village head, the policemen, and the United Youth Corps members before being directed

추녀 끝에 매달아 두었던 것으로 학교 운동회 때마다 비둘기들을 넣은 대바구니 두 개를 맞붙여 얇은 종이를 발라 만든 큰 공을 높이 매달아 놓은 데 사용되던 거였다. 그것은 얼마나 신나는 경기였던가. 청백으로 나뉜 우리들이 모래 넣어 꿰맨 헝겊 공(오제미)을 던져 상대편 바구니를 먼저 터뜨리는 순간 비둘기들이 날고 머리 위로 오색 테이프가 흘러내리고 색종이가 나부낄 때 기분이란. 그런데 바구니 공을 매달아 놓던 장대가 이런 엉뚱한 데 쓰일 줄이야. 장대 두 개는 이제 한쪽에 몰려 있는 사람을 울타리에서 떼어 내서 내모는 구실을 했다. 장대 양 끝에 군인 한 사람씩 붙어서 군중 속으로 끌고 들어가 장대로 오십 명쯤을 뚝 떼어 내어 교문 밖으로 내몰아 가는 것이었다.

이런 와중을 틈타 길수 형과 나는 사람들 사이로 빠져나와 할머니가 있는 조회대 뒤편으로 냅다 뛰어갔다. 청년단원들이 우리 다리를 겨냥해서 대창을 아래로 휘둘렀다. 그러나 용케 맞지 않았다. 우리가 쫓기며 조회대 뒤로 가자 거기 모인 우익 인사 가족들이 얼른 우리를 안으로 끌어넣어 주었다. 할머니가 달려들어 치마를 벌리고 닭이 병아리 품듯이 우리를 싸서 숨겼다. 우리 뒤를 쫓던 청년단원 두 명이 우리를 포기한 것은 마침 우리 뒤미처 달려

to sit down behind the podium.

"I sensed that something was up, so I found my mother and we mingled with the group of military families coming forward. With my brother-in-law being in the military, we didn't exactly qualify as immediate family, but fortunately Mr. Kang, the Village Head, looked the other way," Uncle said.

"That's what I mean, Older Brother. What, if anything, did it cost you to hand your sister over to me, after all that 'over-my-dead-body' protest about her marrying a northerner?" Uncle-in-law cut in with a chuckle.

The police families came forward next, followed by public officials' families. By then, sensing something ominous, the crowd was starting to get restless. When it was finally the turn for the families of the United Youth Corps members and the executives of the National Assembly, people elbowed their way and tripped over each other to go up and plead with the Village Head and the Youth Corps members.

"Chŏng-suk's father, don't you know my brother back home joined the army last year?"

"Look, Village Head, sir, my cousin is a policeman at the Kŭmnyŏng Police Substation. His name is

드는 다른 사람들 때문이었으리라. 아이들과 아낙네 열 명쯤이 달려들었다가 마구 내지르는 대창에 쫓겨 갔다.

장대 두 개가 서로 번갈아가며 사람들을 몰아갔다. 장대가 머리 위로 떨어질 때마다 사람들은 비명을 지르며 뒤로 나자빠지고 장대에 걸린 사람들은 빠져나오려고 허우적거렸다. 장대 뒤에서 빠져나오려는 사람들에게 몽둥이를 휘두르고 공포를 쏘아대자 사람들은 장대에 떠밀려 주춤주춤 교문 밖으로 걸어 나갔다. 교문 밖에 맞바로 잇닿은 일주 도로에 내몰린 사람들은 모두 한결같이 길바닥에 주저앉아 울며불며 살려 달라고 애걸했다. 군인들의 바짓가랑이를 붙잡고 울부짖는 할머니들, 총부리에 등을 찔려 앞으로 곤두박질치는 아낙네들, 군인들은 총구로 찌르고 개머리판을 사정없이 휘둘렀다. 사람들은 휘둘러대는 총개머리판이 무서워 엉금엉금 기어갔다. 가면 죽는 줄 번연히 알면서 어떻게 제 발로 서서 걸어가겠는가. 뒤처지는 사람들에게는 뒤꿈치에다 대고 총을 쏘아댔다.

군인들이 이렇게 돼지 몰듯 사람들을 몰고 우리 시야 밖으로 사라지고 나면 얼마 없어 일제사격 총소리가 콩 볶듯이 일어나곤 했다. 통곡 소리가 천지를 진동했다. 할머니도 큰아버지도 길수 형도 나도 울었다. 우익 인사 가

Kim Kap-jae, you know."

"Step back. None of you qualify as immediate family. Back off," the Village Head waved his hand.

"What do you mean by immediate family?"

"Please, let me in, Village Head, sir."

In the middle of this chaotic commotion, a sudden sharp cry rose from the crowd.

"Fire! The village is on fire!"

The crowd, stunned, rushed to the rock wall surrounding the schoolyard and climbed on top.

"It's fire, fire."

"There's fire, there's fire."

"Oh, no. Oh, no."

Cries and screams erupted from all sides of the schoolyard, rising in a whirlwind and piercing the sky. I didn't have to run to the wall to clearly see sparks flying in the blackened sky east of the village. The stinging smell of smoke began to blow in more and more. At that point, the western rock wall caved in under the weight of all the people clinging to it. As soon as they swarmed around the opening in the wall, trying to escape, the guns went off. The crowd ran back to the middle of the yard. An elder in a white cotton jacket and brown pants was lying on the rubble of the wall, face down, motionless

족들도 넋 놓고 엉엉 울고 있었다. 우는 것은 사람만이 아니었다. 마을에서 외양간에 매인 채 불에 타 죽는 소 울음소리와 말 울음소리도 처절하게 들려왔다. 중낮부터 시작된 이런 아수라장은 저물녘까지 지긋지긋하게 계속되었다. 길수 형이 말했다.

"그때 혼자 살아난 순이삼촌 허는 말을 들으난, 군인들이 일주도로변 옴팡진 밭에다가 사름들을 밀어붙였는디, 사름마다 밭이 안 들어가젠 밭담 우엔 엎디어젼 이마빡을 쪼사 피를 찰찰 흘리멍 살려 달렌 하던 모양입디다."

"쯧쯧쯧, 운동장에 벳겨져 널려진 임자 없는 고무신을 다 모아 놓으면 아매도 가매니로 하나는 실히 되었을 거여. 죽은 사람 몇백 명이나 되카?" 하고 작은당숙이 말하자 길수 형은 낯을 모질게 찌푸리며 말을 씹어뱉었다.

"면에서는 이 집에 고구마 몇 가마 내고 저 집에 유채 몇 가마 소출냈는지는 알아가도 그날 죽은 사람 수효는 이날 이때 한 번도 통계 잡아 보지 않으니, 내에 참. 내 생각엔 오백 명은 넘은 것 같은디, 한 육백 명 안 되카 마씸? 한 번에 오륙십 명씩 열한 번에 몰아가시니까."

열한 번째로 끌려가던 사람들은 그야말로 운수 대통한 사람들이었다. 때마침 대대장 차가 도착하여 총살 중지

and apparently lifeless. About a dozen soldiers swiftly jumped onto the wall and aimed their rifles downward. The twenty plus soldiers standing in a double line behind the podium quickly broke ranks with their rifles held close to their chests and surrounded the crowd from the front. The officer on the podium raised his pistol above his shoulder and threatened the villagers. When he turned his chin up forcefully, his helmet sparkled in the sunlight.

"Listen carefully. We are in the process of carrying out an operation. Your houses are being incinerated in accordance with orders. As our next mission is to transport you evacuees to Jeju City, I want you to remember that anyone who behaves in a disorderly manner during the evacuation will be executed without hesitation, just as in the previous incident."

His crisp metallic voice with the alien Northern accent reverberated over the heads of the terrified villagers. Doubtful that they were being evacuated to Jeju City, they tried to read the faces of the soldiers. What premonition so terrified them that they even forgot to despair at their homes going up in flames? The choking smell of smoke, carried on the sea breeze blowing in from the village, was getting stronger, and the red haze was shimmering in a sky

명령을 내렸던 것이다. 이 불행한 사건에도 예외 없이 '만약'이란 가정이 따라왔다. 만약 대대장이 읍에서부터 타고 오던 찝차가 도중에 고장만 나지 않았더라면 한 시간 더 일찍 도착했을 터이고, 그렇게 되면 삼백 명이나 사백 명은 더 살렸을 것이다. 따라서 희생자는 백 명 내외로 줄어들 것이고, 또 적에게 오염됐다고 판단된 부락을 토벌해서 백 명 정도의 이적 행위자를 사살했다면 그건 수긍할 만한 일이었을지 모른다. 그러나 피살자 육백 명이란 수효는 옥석을 가리지 않은 무차별 사격을 의미했다.

"고모부님, 대대장이 말한 차 고장은 핑계가 아닐까 마씸? 일개 중대장이 대대장도 모르게 어떻게 그런 엄청난 일을 저지를 수가 이서 마씸?"

고모부는 그 당시 토벌군으로 애월면에 가 있었기 때문에 자세한 것은 알지 못할 터였다. 고모부는 한때 인근 부락인 함덕리에 주둔했던 서북청년으로만 구성된 중대에 소속되어 있었는데 마침 사건 수개월 전에 애월로 이동해 갔던 것이었다. 신혼 초라 고모도 따라갔었다.

"그 당시엔 중대장 즉결처분권이란 것이 있을 때랐쥬. 또 갸들이 전투사령부의 작전 명령에 따라 행동했댄 해도 작전 명령을 잘못 해석하였을 공산이 커. 난 졸병 군대 생

black with airborne ashes. Besides, we could hear sporadic gunfire.

"I was coming back from West Village that day where I had gone to bargain for a cow. When I reached the grove of short pine trees on Pille Hill, I looked down and saw the former Village Chief's place and Chong-ju's house on fire. Hiding in the pine grove, I watched soldiers going from house to house using burning millet straw for torches and setting fire to the eaves of the houses."

When people began to line up facing the school gate as ordered by the soldiers, the message "the soldiers are going kill us" suddenly ran through the crowd like an electric current. In no time, those at the head of the line closest to the gate scrambled toward the back of the line. The officer at the podium, brandishing his gun, yelled at the top of his lungs that those retreating would be shot on the spot with no mercy. They paused at his warning only for a moment before starting to retreat again.

At this point, my Uncle said with a long sigh, "My God, I can't tell you how frantically I was looking for our two boys, Kil-su and (referring to me) Sang-su. Mother and I shouted as loud as we could, but they were nowhere to be seen..."

활해서 잘은 모르지만 아마 그것도 견벽청야 작전의 일부일 거라. 쉬운 말로 소개 작전이란 거쥬. 견벽청야 작전이란 것이 뭐냐믄 손자병법에서 따온 것이라는데, 공비를 소탕할 때 먼저 토벌군으로 벽을 쌓아 병풍을 만들고 그 후 들을 말끔히 청소하는 거라. 산간벽촌을 일일이 다 보호헐 수 없는 것 아니냔 말이여. 그러니 일정한 거점만 확보하고 나머지 지역은 인원과 물자를 비워 버려 공비가 발붙일 여지가 없게 하자는 궁리이었쥬. 그런디 인원과 물자를 비워 버리라는 대목에서 그만 잘못 일이 글러진 거라. 작전 지역 내의 인원과 물자를 안전지역으로 후송하라는 뜻이 인원을 전원 총살하고 물자를 전부 소각하라는 것으로 둔갑하고 말았이니 말이여."

"아니, 고모부님도 참, 그 말을 곧이 들엄수꽈? 그건 웃대가리들이 책임을 모면해 보젠 둘러대는 핑계라 마씸. 우리 부락처럼 떼죽음당한 곳이 한둘이 아니고 이 섬을 뺑 돌아가멍 수없이 많은데 그게 다 작전 명령을 잘못 해석해서 일어난 사건이란 말이우꽈? 말도 안 되는 소리우다. 이 작전 명령 자체가 작전 지역의 민간인을 전부 총살하라는 게 틀림없어 마씸."

"겔쎄, 나도 중산간 부락민들을 해안 지방으로 소개시

Though we heard Grandmother and Uncle taking turns yelling out our names, we couldn't find our way out, caught up in the crowd milling in confusion. Crying and barefoot, having lost our rubber shoes, we were being shoved this way and pushed that way.

We held hands tightly and never let go of each other. The schoolyard was utter pandemonium with villagers crying and calling for family members and enraged soldiers cursing and swearing.

At that moment the thunderous bang of a single gunshot exploded above our heads. With a collective "Oh!" people ran en masse and pressed themselves against the western wall. Silence fell instantly upon the yard like a wet blanket. In the space just vacated by the crowd a woman was lying still on her stomach, a baby thrown to her side. The baby was crying as hysterically and loudly as it possibly could in the otherwise absolute stillness.

"Yŏng-bae's wife is shot!" someone whispered.

The bright red blots of fresh blood were striking against her white jacket.

"That two-year-old baby was none other than Chang-shik who owns and runs the mill. His grandmother raised him afterward. Given that he's not

키는 데 참가했었쥬마는…… 겔쎄 말이여, 일단 몇 날 몇 시까지 소개하라고 포고령이 내린 후제도 계속 작전 지역에 남아 있는 자는 공비나 공비 동조자로 간주해서 노인, 아이 할 거 없이 전부 사살하라는 명령은 있었쥬. 사실 작전 지역 내의 어떤 부락에 들어서민, 바로 전날에 두 집 건너서 하나씩 붙여 놔둔 소개하라는 포고문이 발기발기 찢어전 바람에 펄럭펄럭하는디, 이건 틀림없이 공비 소굴이구나 하는 생각이 팍 들어라. 그런디 이 부락 사건은 소개하라고 사전에 포고령도 없어시니……."

그러나 작전 명령에 의해 소탕된 것은 거개가 노인과 아녀자들이었다. 그러니 군경 쪽에서 찾던 소위 도피자들도 못되는 사람들이었다. 그런 사람들에게 총질을 하다니! 또 도피 생활을 하느라고 마침 마을을 떠나 있어서 화를 면했던 남정네들이 군경을 피해 다녔으니까 도피자가 틀림없겠지만 그들도 공비는 아니었다. 사실 그들은 문자 그대로, 공비에게도 쫓기고 군경에게도 쫓겨 할 수 없이 이리저리 피해 도망 다니는 도피자일 따름이었다.

그런데도 군경 측에서는 왜 도피자를 공비와 동일시했던가? 아마 그건 한때 무식한 부락민들이 저지른 섣부른 과오 때문이었나 보다. 5·10 선거 때 부락 출신 몇몇 공산

only married but also has produced two sons for a family that was all but annihilated, his slain mother must have been watching over him, I'd say," Younger Tangsuk commented.

At the sight of a dead body I froze with fear. I couldn't muster the courage to run behind the podium where the officer was standing with his drawn gun, even though the crowd had withdrawn and there was nothing standing in my way. That man would most definitely shoot at us if we moved in that direction. We didn't know what to do other than fidget desperately.

As the crowd stuck close to the west wall, refusing to come forward, soldiers brought out two long bamboo poles. These poles were kept hanging from the eaves in front of the teachers' office, except during a school athletic event when they were used to hoist large balls, each made of two round, woven bamboo-baskets glued together and covered with thin paper to make a sphere containing doves. How exciting that game was. Split into two teams, Blue and White, we would throw small cloth bags loosely filled with sand at the other team's ball in order to break it open first. How wonderful that moment was when the doves flew out, streams of rainbow-

주의 골수분자의 선동에 부화뇌동하여 선거를 보이콧한 사건이 화근이 된 것이었다. 그것이 두고두고 군경 측에 부락을 적색시하는 빌미가 될 줄이야. 부락민들이 아무리 개과천선하여 결백을 내보여도 소용이 없었다. 부락민들이 5·10 선거 보이콧을 선동했던 주모자 한라산 입산 공비 김진배의 아내를 부락에서 추방하고, 그의 밭 한가운데를 파헤쳐, 비 오면 물 차는 못을 만들면서까지 결백을 주장했으나, 군경의 오해는 막무가내였다.

밤에는 부락 출신 공비들이 나타나 입산하지 않는 자는 반동이라고 대창으로 찔러 죽이고, 낮에는 함덕리의 순경들이 스리쿼터를 타고 와 도피자 검속을 하니, 결국 마을 남정들은 낮이나 밤이나 숨어 지낼 수밖에 없는 처지였다. 순경들이 도피자라고 찾던 폐병쟁이 종철이 형은 공비가 습격해 온 밤에 궤 뒤에 숨어 있다가 기침을 몹시 하는 바람에 발각되어 대창에 찔려 죽었고 헛간 멍석 세워 둔 틈에 숨어 있다가 역시 공비의 대창 맞고 죽은 완식이 아버지도 순경들이 찾던 도피자였다. 우리 종조부님도 사건 석 달 전에 부락 출신 공비의 대창에 찔려 돌아가셨다. 당시 1구 구장이던 종조부님은 밤중에 내려온 마을 출신 폭도들로부터 식량을 모아 달라는 요구에 고개를 흔들었

colored ribbons tumbled down on our heads, and confetti fluttered everywhere. Who would have thought that those same bamboo poles would be put to such a strange use: removing people from a wall. Soldiers, one at each end of a pole, knocked off about fifty people, and drove them out through the schoolyard gate.

Taking advantage of this chaos, Cousin Kil-su and I managed to slip through the crowd and dash to Grandmother behind the podium. Members of the Youth Corps swung their bamboo spears low, aiming at our legs. Fortunately they missed. As soon as we were chased behind the podium, the right-wing families gathered there swiftly pulled us into their group. Grandmother rushed to us and, with her long skirt spread wide, wrapped and hid us like a hen embracing her chicks. Maybe because others dashed to follow us, the two Youth Corps members who had been hounding us gave up. About ten children and women rushed to join the group, only to be chased away by Youth Corp members swinging their bamboo spears wildly.

Meanwhile, the two bamboo poles took turns herding the villagers. Each time a pole fell on their heads, people screamed and dropped onto their

던 것이다.

"그렇게는 못 해여. 쌀을 모아도랜 허지 말앙 차라리 빼앗앙가게. 자진해서 쌀 모아 주었다가 냉중에 경찰에서 알민 우린 어떵 되는가. 숭시가 나고말고. 그러니 제발 부탁햄시메 쌀을 모아 도랜 말앙 억지로 빼앗앙가게."

이렇게 협조 못하겠다는 말에 화가 난 폭도들은 그 자리에서 가슴팍에 대창을 내질렀던 것이었다. 같은 날 밤 용케 약탈을 면했던 철동이네 집은, 약탈당하지 않은 것으로 보아 필시 공비와 내통함에 틀림없다는 엉뚱한 오해를 받아, 이튿날 경찰에게 화를 당했다.

나는 한밤중 밖에서 대창으로 창호지창을 퍽 찌르며 "모두 잠깨라. 우리가 왔다!" 하고 무섭게 속삭이던 목소리와 뒤미처 아버지의 겁먹은 얼굴 위에 쏟아지던 덴찌불을 생각하면 지금도 몸이 오싹해진다.

이렇게 안팎으로 혹독하게 부대낀 마을 남정들 중에는 아버지처럼 여러 달 전에 밤중에 통통배를 타고 일본으로 밀항해 버린 사람도 있고 육지 전라도 땅으로 피신하는 사람도 있었다. 어떤 집에서는 아무래도 불길한 예감이 들었던지 사내아이들을 다른 마을로 보내기도 했다. 그것도 큰놈은 읍내 이모네 집에, 샛놈(가운데 아들)은 함덕 외

backs, and while others who were trapped struggled to escape, only to be met with flying clubs and the firing of blanks, some were pushed out the schoolyard gate, resisting all the way. Shoved onto the loop road right beyond the gate, they all sat down, weeping and begging for mercy. Grandmothers were crying and clinging to the legs of soldiers, while younger women jabbed in the back by gun barrels were falling down. Without remorse, the soldiers kept prodding them with muzzles and whacking them with rifle butts. People crawled on their hands and knees trying to avoid the ruthlessly swung rifles. How could anyone expect them to walk on their own two feet knowing without a doubt that they were being marched to their own deaths? Shots were fired at the heels of any who fell behind.

Shortly after the soldiers herded each group like pigs and they disappeared, a volley of gunfire would erupt like corn popping. Wails shook the earth and filled the air. Grandmother, Uncle, Cousin Kil-su, and I were all crying. The right-wing families were also weeping loudly and wildly. It wasn't only people that were screaming. Cows and horses, tethered inside barns in the village were also howling,

삼촌한테, 막내 놈은 또 어디에 하는 식으로 사방에 뿔뿔이 흩어 놓았다. 그건 아마도 한군데 모여 있다가 몰살되어 씨멸족하면 종자 하나 추리지 못할까 봐 생각해 낸 궁리였으리라.

그러나 대부분의 남정네들은 마을에 그대로 눌러 있었는데, 이들은 폭도에 쫓기고 군경에 쫓겨 갈팡질팡하다가, 결국은 할 수 없이 한라산 아래의 목장으로 올라가 마른 냇가의 굴속에 피난했다. 행방을 알 길 없는 남편 때문에 모진 고문을 당하던 순이삼촌도 따라 올라갔다. 이 섬은 워낙 화산 지대라 곳곳에 동굴이 뚫려 있어서, 우리 부락처럼 폭도에도 쫓기고 군경에도 쫓긴 양민들이 몰래 숨어 있기 안성맞춤이었다.

솥도 져 나르고 이불도 가져갔다. 밥을 지을 때 연기가 나면 발각될까 봐 연기 안 나는 청미래 덩굴로 불을 땠다. 청미래 덩굴은 비에도 젖지 않아 땔감으로는 십상이었다. 잠은 밥 짓고 난 잉걸불 위에 굵은 나무때기를 얼기설기 얹어 침상처럼 만들고 그 위에서 잤다. 쌀은 아끼고 들판에 널려 까마귀밥이나 되고 있는 썩은 말고기를 주워다 먹었다. 겨울이 되어도 난리 때문에 미처 내리지 못한 소와 말이 목장에는 좀 남아 있었는데 그냥 놔두면 한라산 공비

letting out desperate, ghastly cries as they burned alive in the fire. The seemingly never-ending horrific mayhem that began at midday kept on going until dusk.

Cousin Kil-su spoke: "According to Sun-i Samch'on, the only survivor of the massacre, as the soldiers were pushing people into the sunken field along the loop route, all of them were resisting, clinging face down to the hedge, begging for their lives with blood gushing from their crushed foreheads."

"*Tsk tsk tsk.* If all the rubber shoes scattered around the schoolyard with no one to claim them had been collected, they would easily have filled an 80-kilogram grain sack. Wonder how many hundreds died?" Younger Tangsuk said, before Cousin Kil-su, with a wry scowl, spoke in a tone of disgust.

"The county officials know how many straw bags of sweet potatoes this household harvested or how many bags of produce that that patch of field yielded, but so far they've failed to come up with the number of people who died that day. It must have been over five hundred, maybe even six hundred? They took fifty to sixty people each time, eleven times total."

The eleventh group was the luckiest, no question

들의 양식이 된다고 토벌군이 총으로 쏘아 죽여, 쇠고기만 운반해 가고 말고기는 그대로 내버려 두었던 것이다.

그러나 천장에서 물이 뚝뚝 떨어지는 혈거 생활은 고생이 말이 아니었다. 이불이 점점 젖어들고 얼어 죽는 사람이 생겼다. 삼 년 뒤 온 섬이 평정되어 할머니를 따라 목장에 고사리 꺾으러 갔다가 비를 만나 어느 동굴로 피해 들어갔을 때, 굴속에 사람의 흰 뼈다귀와 흰 고무신을 보고 얼마나 놀랐는지 모른다.

하여튼 이렇게 남정네들이 마을을 비우자 군경 측에서는 자연히 입산한 것으로 오해하게 되고 그러한 오해가 저 섣달 열여드레의 끔찍한 사건의 소지가 되었음은 말할 것도 없다. 그 사건은 마을 남정들이 그 냇가 동굴에서 혈거 생활을 시작한 지 아흐레 만에 일어난 것이었다. 그런데 하필 그날 순이삼촌은 우리 할머니에게 맡겨 두었던 오누이 자식을 데리러 내려와 있다가 그만 화를 당하고 만 것이었다.

문득 길수 형의 열띤 목소리가 방 안을 울렸다.

"하여간에 이 사건은 그냥 넘어갈 수 없우다. 아명해도 밝혀 놔야 됩니다. 두 번 다시 이런 일이 안 생기도록 경종을 울리는 뜻에서라도 꼭 밝혀 두어야 합니다. 그 학살

about it. Just in time, the battalion commander's vehicle arrived to order an end to the shooting. Not surprisingly, this deplorable event entailed its own what-ifs. If the battalion commander's vehicle hadn't broken down on the way from the center of the county, it would have arrived an hour earlier and three to four hundred more lives would have been spared, reducing the number of victims to less than a hundred. If they had subjugated a village they thought was infiltrated by the enemy and executed about a hundred traitors who were assisting that enemy, it might have been understandable. But for six hundred people to have been executed simply meant that they were shooting indiscriminately without sorting the wheat from the chaff.

"Uncle, don't you think the "breakdown" of the battalion commander's car was just a lame excuse? How could a mere company commander carry out an enormous operation like that without the battalion commander knowing?"

It was unlikely that Uncle, who, as part of the subjugating force, had been sent to Aewŏl Township, had any firsthand knowledge about how exactly the incident came about. His company, which consisted exclusively of members of the Northwest Youth

이 상부의 작전 명령이었는지 그 중대장의 독자적 행동이었는지 누구의 잘잘못인지 하여간 밝혀 내야 합니다. 우린 그 중대장 이름도 모르는 형편 아니우꽈?"

이 말에 큰당숙어른이 고개를 절레절레 흔들었다.

"거 무신 쓸데없는 소리고! 이름은 알아 무싱거(무엇) 허젠? 다 시국 탓이엔 생각하고 말지 공연시리 긁엉 부스럼 맹글 거 없저."

고모부도 맞장구쳤다.

"하여간 그 작자들이 아직 퍼렇게 살아 있는 동안은 아마 어려울 거여. 그것들이 우리가 그 문제를 들고 나오게 가만 놔둠직해여? 또 삼십 년 묵은 일이니 형법상 범죄 구성도 안 될 터이고."

그러나 길수 형은 자기 주장을 꺾지 않았다.

"아니우다. 이대로 그냥 놔두민 이 사건은 영영 매장되고 말 거우다. 앞으로 일이십 년만 더 있어 봅서. 그땐 심판받을 당사자도 죽고 없고, 아버님이나 당숙님같이 증언할 분도 돌아가시고 나민 다 허사가 아니우꽈? 마을 전설로는 남을지 몰라도."

길수 형의 말에 갑자기 짜증이 났던지 고모부의 입에서 느닷없이 평안도 사투리가 튀어나왔다.

Corps, used to be stationed in Hamdŏk Village but moved to Aewŏl a few months before the event. My aunt, newly married to him, followed.

"At that time, a company commander had the authority to enforce orders and carry out summary executions. Even if the company was following orders of the combat battalion commander, they probably misinterpreted them. I can't say for sure since I served in the army as a lowly foot soldier, but what happened must have been part of the Surround-and-Cleanse field maneuver. In layman's terms, it's an evacuation tactic directly borrowed from The Art of War by Sun Tzu: when eradicating guerillas, you have to surround the area with force like a wall and then empty the field. You couldn't possibly guard each and every remote village in the hills. So the idea is, once you've secured certain strategic positions, you empty the remaining areas of human and material resources so that no guerillas can establish a foothold. But a mistake was made in the clearing of human and material resources. What was supposed to be an evacuation of people and resources from the area of operation to a safe zone somehow turned into the execution of the entire population and the destruction, by fire, of all resources."

"기쎄, 조캐, 지나간 걸 개지구 자꾸 들춰내선 멀하간? 전쟁이란 다 기런 거이 아니가서?"

순간 오십줄 나이의 고모부 얼굴에서 삼십 년 전의 새파란 서북청년의 모습을 힐끗 엿본 느낌이 들었다. 가슴이 섬뜩했다. 야릇한 반발감이 뾰죽하게 일어났다.

내 아래 또래의 아이들에게 몰래 양과자를 주어 아버지나 형이 숨은 곳을 가르쳐 달라고 꾀어내던 서청 출신의 순경들, 철모르는 아이들은 대밭에서, 마루 밑에서, 외양간 밑이나 조짚가리 밑을 판 굴에서 여러 번 제 아버지와 형을 가리켜 냈다. 도피자 아들을 찾아내라고 여든 살 노인을 닦달하던 어떤 서청 순경은 대답 안 한다고 어린 손자를 총으로 위협해서 무릎 꿇고 앉은 제 할아버지의 따귀를 때리도록 강요했다. 닭 잡아 내라고 공포를 빵빵 쏘아대기도 했다. 그들은 또 여맹이 뭣 하는지도 모르는 무식한 촌처녀들을 붙잡아다가 공연히 여맹에 가입했다는 혐의를 뒤집어씌우고 발가벗겨 놓고 눈요기를 일삼았다. 순이삼촌도 그런 식으로 당했다. 지서에 붙들어다 놓고 남편의 행방을 대라는 닦달 끝에 옷을 벗겼다는 것이었다. 어이없게도 그건 간밤에 남편이 왔다 갔는지 알아본다는 핑계였는데, 남편이 왔다 갔으면 분명 그 짓을 했을

"Oh Uncle, come now, do you really believe all that? It was only some excuse the higher ups invented to duck responsibility. There were countless villages like ours all over the island where much of the population got slaughtered. Are you saying it was all an accident resulting from misunderstanding an order? That's ludicrous. I have no doubt that the order was to execute all civilians in the area of operation."

"Well, I also took part in evacuating mid-mountain villagers to the coastal areas... Now you see, there was indeed an order to treat as a guerilla or guerilla sympathizer and shoot to kill anybody, including the elderly and children, who remained after the order to evacuate by D-day H-hour was posted. In fact, in some villages we entered, we'd find the evacuation decrees we had posted on every third house the night before ripped up and flapping in the wind. Then we assumed right away that those places were obviously guerilla strongholds. But this village was never warned by any evacuation decree..."

Yet most of those killed during the operation were the elderly, women, and children. They bore no resemblance to the so-called escapees that the mili-

것이고, 아직 거기엔 분명 그 흔적이 남아 있을 테니 들여다보자는 것이었다. 나는, 어느 날 마당에서 도리깨질하던 순이삼촌이 남편의 행방을 안 댄다고 빼앗긴 도리깨로 머리가 깨어지도록 얻어맞는 광경을 내 눈으로 직접 본 적이 있었다.

거기다가 이들은 밭에서 혼자 김매는 젊은 여자만 보면 무조건 냅다 덮친다는 소문이었으니 나이 찬 딸을 둔 집에서는 이래저래 여간 불안한 게 아니었다. 그러니 딸이 겁탈당하기를 기다리느니 미리 선수를 써서 서청 출신 군인에게 시집보낸 우리 할아버지의 처사는 백 번 잘한 일이었다. 아직 스무 살 어린 나이에 별 분수를 모르던 고모부는 할아버지가 꾀로 어르는 바람에 얼떨결에 결혼하고 만 것이었는데 고모는 고모부보다 두 살이 더 많았다.

하여간 그 당시 도피자 가족들 중에는 목숨을 부지해 보려는 방편으로 이런 정략결혼이 성행했는데, 그것은 연대가 교체되어 육지로 떠남에 따라 거의 파경에 이르고 애비 없는 자식들만 서럽게 자라고 있었음은 물론이다. 그러나 우리 고모부는 역시 할아버지가 잘 보아 고른 사람이라 그랬는지 휴전과 더불어 처가를 다시 찾아 입도한 후 지금까지 삼십 년간 이 고장 사람이 되어 살아온 것이

tary and police were searching for. And they were gunned down indiscriminately! What's more, those young men who dodged the catastrophe by staying away from the village weren't guerillas in any sense of the word, though maybe they could have been considered "escapees." But they were escapees only in the sense that they were forced to run from place to place, trying to escape being hunted down by both sides, the guerillas and the military police.

Why did the military and police still see escapees and guerillas in the same light? Maybe because of an unfortunate decision the villagers once made, out of ignorance. Maybe the root of the evil was the boycott of the May 10 election by the villagers, who blindly followed a handful of hard-core communist agitators among themselves. Who would have guessed that this boycott would provide a pretext for the military and police to brand and treat the village as a communist stronghold for a long, long time? Nothing the villagers did to demonstrate their innocence made any difference. For example, they expelled from the village the wife of Kim Chin-bae, the Mt. Halla guerilla agitator who led the boycott. They went so far as to band together and dig up the middle of his field, so it turned into a useless pond

었다. 이러한 고모부가 방정맞게 갑자기 이북 사투리를 쓰다니. 고모부의 느닷없는 이북 사투리는 좌중의 다른 분들에게도 이런 것들을 일깨워 주었는지 잠시 침묵이 흘렀다.

벌써 멧밥을 짓는지 부엌에서 마른 솔가지 태우는 매운 냄새가 마루를 건너 흘러들어 왔다. 고샅길로 지나다니는 사람들의 말소리가 두런두런 들려왔다. 아마 한 집 제사를 끝내고 다른 집으로 옮아가는 사람들이리라.

고모부는 다른 사람들 귀에 거슬리는 줄도 모르고 다시 이북 사투리로 말을 꺼냈다.

"도민들이 아직도 서청을 안 좋게 생각하구 있디만, 조캐네들 생각해 보라마. 서청이 와 부모 형제들 니북에 놔둔 채 월남해 왔갔서? 하도 빨갱이 등쌀에 못니겨서 삼팔선을 넘은 거이야. 우린 빨갱이라문 무조건 이를 갈았디. 서청의 존재 이유는 앳세 반공이 아니갔어. 우리레 무데기로 엘에스티(LST) 타구 입도한 건 남로당 천지인 이 섬에 반공 전선을 구축하재는 목적이었디. 우리레 현지에서 입대해설라무니 순경두 되구 군인두 되었디. 기런디 말이야, 우리가 입대해 보니끼니 경찰이나 군대나 영 엉망이드랬어. 군기두 문란하구 남로당 빨갱이들이 득실거리구

when it rained, but the military and police were unrelenting.

At night, guerillas from the village would show up and kill with their bamboo spears 'reactionaries' who refused to follow them into the mountains, while during the day police from Hamdŏk Village drove in to search for escapees. As a result, young male villagers had no choice but to go into hiding. Chong-ch'ŏl, a tuberculosis patient the police were looking for was stabbed and killed by guerillas when they raided the village one night and discovered him hiding behind a grain chest, having a coughing fit. Wan-shik's father, who died by the guerillas' bamboo spears while hiding between rolls of straw mats in the barn, was also an escapee that the police were hunting for. My great-uncle died, three months before the event, stabbed by a guerilla from the village. As the chief of District 1, he refused to give in to the demand for food made by a mob of ex-villagers who had come down from their mountain hideouts in the middle of the night.

"I can't do that. Don't ask me to collect rice for you. I would prefer for you to take it by force. What will happen to us when the police find out that we voluntarily collected rice for you? We'd be dealt

말이야. 전국적으로 안 그랜 향토부대가 없댔디만 특히 이 섬이 심하단 평판이 나 있드랬다. 이 섬 출신 젊은이를 주축으로 창설된 향토 부대에 연대장 암살이 생기디 않나, 반란이 일어나 백여 명이 한꺼번에 입산해설라무니 공비들과 합세해 버리디 않나…… 그 백여 명 빠져나간 공백을 우리 서청이 들어가 메꾸었다. 기래서 우린 첨버텀 섬 사람에 대해서 아주 나쁜 선입견을 개지구 있댔어. 서청뿐만이가서? 야, 그땐 다 기랬어. 후에 교체해개지구 들어온 다른 눅지 향토 부대두 매한가지래서. 사실 그때 눅지 사람치구 이 섬사람들을 도매금으로 몰아쳐 빨갱이루다 보지 않는 사람이 없댔다. 4·3 폭동이 일어나디, 5·10 선거를 방해해설라무니 남한에서 유일하게 이 섬만 선거를 못 치렀디, 군대는 반란이 일어나디. 하이간 이런 북새통이었으니끼니…….”

이때 큰아버지가 끙 앓는 소릴 내며 고개를 돌려 외면해 버렸다. 눈썹이 발에 밟힌 송충이처럼 꿈틀거리는 것으로 보아 몹시 심기가 뒤틀린 모양이었다. 고모부는 그제야 이북 사투리를 쓰고 있는 자신을 깨달았던지 흠칫 놀라며 말을 멈췄다. 큰당숙, 작은당숙 어른도 못마땅한 표정으로 담배만 풀썩풀썩 빨아댔다. 잠시 거북살스러운

with severely, no doubt. So please, I'm begging you, take it by force instead of asking us to collect it."

Outraged by his refusal to cooperate, the mob stabbed him in the chest with their bamboo spears right then and there. Ch'ŏl-dong's family, fortunate to avoid the looting that night, were punished the next day by police who misconstrued their lucky survival as evidence of a secret pact with the guerillas.

I still get chills down my spine when I think of that terrifying midnight whisper, "Wake up, all of you. We're here!" as bamboo spears stabbed at the window paper from outside, followed by a flash of light that would flood my father's frightened face.

Some male villagers brutalized by the left and the right had fled to Japan some months before on smuggled motorboats at midnight, just like my father. Others escaped to Chŏlla Province on the mainland. Maybe heeding dire premonition, some families sent their boys to other villages. They even scattered them in all directions, sending the oldest one to an aunt in town, the middle one to an uncle in Hamdŏk, the youngest to some other home, and so on. It was obviously an attempt to prevent the

침묵이 흘렀다. 그러나 언제나 반죽 좋은 고모부는 곧 섬사투리로 돌아와 다시 말을 꺼냈다.

"성님, 서청이 잘했다는 말이 절대 아니우다. 서청도 참말 욕먹을 건 먹어야 헙쥬. 그런디 이 섬사람을 나쁘게 본 건 서청만이 아니랐우다. 육지 사람치고 그 당시 그런 생각 안 가진 사람이 없어서 마씸. 그렇지 않아도 육지 사람들이 이 섬사람이랜 허민 얕이 보는 편견이 있는디다가 이런 오해가 생겨 부러시니…… 내에 참."

"맞는 말이라. 그땐 온 섬이 육지 것들 독판이랐쥬." 하고 큰당숙어른이 혀를 찼다.

"그때 함덕 지서 주임이 본도 사람이랐는디 부하들한티 명령 없이 도피자를 총살 말렌 당부했는디도 그 육지 것들이 자기 주임이 제주 사람이라고 얕이 보안 함부로 총질했쥬."

이 말에 작은당숙이 한 손을 내저으며 이의를 달았다.

"박 주임이 참말 그런 말을 해서까 마씸? 아매도 죄 없는 사람 죽인 책임을 조금이라도 벗어 보젠 변명허는 걸 거우다."

현모 형도 한마디 거들었다.

"난 들으니까 박 주임 그 사람이 서청보다 되리어 더 악

family from being annihilated without an heir to continue its name.

Nevertheless, the vast majority of men and boys stayed in the village until they were so hounded by the violent mob and the military and police they had no choice but to flee to the meadow at the base of Mt. Halla and hide in the caves along the dried-up riverbed. Having been brutally tortured because of her missing husband, Sun-i Samch'on followed them there. The natural caves all over this volcanic island provided an ideal refuge for people hiding from the mob and the military and police.

Pots and pans were lugged up to the caves, and blankets, too. Smokeless blueberry vine was used for firewood, so there was no cooking smoke. Blueberry vine is also handy because it doesn't get damp in the rain. People slept on makeshift beds of thick twigs roughly tied together above coals from the cooking fire. In order to conserve rice, they collected the rotten horsemeat strewn across the meadow and picked at by crows. Not all the farm animals had been brought back to the village from the meadow before winter because of the disturbance. The police shot the cows and horses left behind, so they wouldn't provide food for the guerillas on Mt.

독하게 놀았댄 헙디다."

고모부가 다시 말을 받았다.

"그것도 그럼직한 말이쥬. 그 당시 본도 출신 순경 중에는 자기네들이 서청헌티 빨갱이로 몰리카부댄 되리어 한 술 더 떠서 과격한 행동으로 나간 사람들이 더러 있어시니까."

"아니라. 나도 잡혀가 취조 받고 풀려나온 인수 아방한티 들은 이야기쥬만, 박 주임은 잡아온 도피자를 여러 사람 몰래 놓아주었댄 해여라. 악독한 것은 그 밑에 있는 육지 것들이라."

사건 후 이 년쯤 뒤에 박 주임은 한 번 부락에 왔다가 치도곤을 당한 일이 있었다. 마침 휴가 중이라 군복 입고 있던 그 감나무 집 청년은 "죽은 우리 아방, 우리 성을 살려내라, 이 사람 백정놈아, 고리 백정놈아!" 하고 부르짖으며 작대기를 휘둘렀던 것이다. 그 인구라는 청년은 현모 형과 한날한시에 입대한 해병대였다.

그 무렵 뒤늦게 초토 작전을 반성하게 된 전투사령부는 선무공작을 펴서 한라산 밑 동굴에 숨은 도피자들을 상당수 귀순시켰는데 현모 형도 그중에 끼여 있었던 것이다. 때마침 6·25가 터져 해병대 모병이 있자 이 귀순자들은

Halla, but they only took the beef, and left behind the horsemeat.

Living in the caves with water constantly dripping from the ceiling was harsh beyond description. As the blankets got soaked, people started dying from hypothermia. I remember, three years later when the whole island had been pacified and we went to the meadow to pick fern brakes, how frightened I was at the sight of white human bones and white rubber shoes in the cave where my grandma and I took shelter from the rain.

Anyhow, the absence of males in the village led the military police to presume, rather understandably, that they had gone into the mountains to join the guerillas. That misinterpretation undoubtedly became the pretext for the terrifying December 18 incident, which occurred on the ninth day after male villagers left for the caves. Sun-i Samch'on came down to the village on that day, of all days, to fetch her son and her daughter whom she had entrusted to my grandma, and got swept up into the disaster.

Abruptly, Cousin Kil-su's impassioned voice rang through the room.

"In any case, we can't just leave this incident

너도나도 입대를 자원했다. 그야말로 빨갱이 누명을 벗을 수 있는 더없이 좋은 기회였다. 그래서 그들은 그대로 눌러 있다간 언제 개죽음할지도 모르는 이 지긋지긋한 고향을 빠져나갈 수 있었던 것이다. 그러니까 현모 형은 인천상륙작전에 참가한 해병대 3기였다. '귀신 잡는 해병'이라고 용맹을 떨쳤던 초창기 해병대는 이렇게 이 섬 출신 청년 삼만 명을 주축으로 이룩된 것이었다. 그러나 그 용맹이란 과연 무엇일까? 그건 따지고 보면 결국 반대급부적인 행위가 아니었을까? 빨갱이란 누명을 뒤집어쓰고 몇 번씩이나 죽을 고비를 넘긴 그들인지라 한 번 여봐란 듯이 용맹을 떨쳐 누명을 벗어 보이고 싶었으리라. 아니, 그것만이 아니다. 어쩌면 거기엔 보복적인 감정이 짙게 깔려 있지 않았을까? 이북 사람에게 당한 것을 이북 사람에게 돌려준다는 식으로 말이다. 섬 청년들이 6·25 동란 때 보인 전사에 빛나는 그 용맹은, 한때 군경 측에서 섬 주민이라면 무조건 좌익시해서 때려잡던 단세포적인 사고방식이 얼마나 큰 오류를 저질렀나를 반증하는 것이 된다.

이런 생각을 하자니 속에서 울화가 불끈 치밀어 올랐다. 기분 같아선 은연중에 서청을 변호하는 고모부를 면박 주고 싶었지만 꾹 눌러 참았다. 그래도 내 말은 약간

behind and move on. Whatever it takes, we should find out exactly what happened. The truth must be brought to light, to prevent something like this from ever happening again, if for no other reason. Whether the massacre was ordered by higher authorities, or was an independent decision by that company commander, we must find out where the blame lies. We don't even know the name of the company commander, do we?"

At this, Older Tangsuk shook his head. "What futility! What would you do with the name if you found it out? It would be better to blame it on the times instead of asking for trouble."

Uncle chimed in. "Anyhow, it won't be easy as long as those individuals are still alive and well. Do you think they'll let us bring this question up in public? Besides, after thirty years, it's too late to prosecute according to criminal law."

But Cousin Kil-su wouldn't give in.

"I disagree. If we leave things as they are, this incident will be buried and forgotten forever. In another decade or two, there will be no one left to put on trial, no witnesses like my father and his cousin. It will all be over, just a village legend."

The P'yŏngan dialect burst from Uncle's mouth, as

서슬져서 나왔다.

"고모부님, 고모분 당시 삼십만 도민 중에 진짜 빨갱이 얼마나 된다고 생각햄수꽈?"

"그것사 만 명쯤 되는 비무장 공비 빼 부리면 얼마 되여? 무장 공비 한 삼백 명쯤 되까?"

이 말에 나도 모르게 발끈 성미가 났다.

"도대체 비무장 공비란 것이 뭐우꽈? 무장도 안 한 사람을 공비라고 할 수 이서 마씸? 그 사람들은 중산간 부락 소각으로 갈 곳 잃어 한라산 밑 여기저기 동굴에 숨어 살던 피난민이우다."

나의 반박하는 말에 고모부는 의외라는 듯이 흠칫 나를 바라보았다.

"그건 서울 조캐 말이 맞아. 나도 직접 내 눈으로 봤쥬. 목장 지대서 작전 중인디 아기 울음소리가 들리길래 덤불 속을 헤쳐 수색해 보난 동굴이 나왔는디 그 속에 비무장 공비 스무남은 명이 들어 있지 않애여."

"비무장 공비가 아니라 피난민이라 마씸."

나는 다시 한번 단호하게 고모부의 말을 수정했다.

"맞아, 내가 말을 자꾸 실수해졈저. 그땐 산에 올라간 사람은 무조건 폭도로 봤이니까. 하이간 굴속에 있는 사

though he was irritated by Cousin Kil-su's remark.

"Now, Nephew, what's the point of digging up again and again what is done and past? Isn't that how things go down in a war?"

For a split second, I thought I glimpsed a youthful Northwest Youth Corps member from thirty years ago in the face of my fifty-something Uncle. A chill raced through my heart. I suddenly felt a sharp pang of resentment.

Furtively handing out Western candies, the Northwest Youth Corps members—turned-police officers would coax kids my age to reveal where their fathers and brothers were hiding. The kids didn't know any better so they pointed time and again to their relatives in the bamboo groves, beneath the paneled floors, or in the tunnels under the cowsheds and among the stacks of millet straw. When an eighty-year-old man refused, under interrogation, to say where his escapee son was, the policeman from the Youth Corps threatened his young grandson with a gun and forced the child to slap his kneeling grandfather in the face. The police would fire blank shots—*bang bang*—and demand fresh chicken dishes. They also routinely ogled the bare bodies of the innocent country girls they

람은 영 행색이 말이 아니라서. 굶언 피골이 상접헌디다가 한겨울에 젖은 미녕옷 한 벌로 몸을 가리고 떨고 있는디, 동상 걸려 발구락 모지라진 사람도 더러 있었쥬. 소위 비무장 공비란 것이 이 모냥으로 동굴 속에서 비참한 꼴로 발견되니까 냉중엔 상부에서도 생각을 달리 쓰게 되어서. 구호물자를 준비한 갱생원 차려 놓고 선무공작을 썼쥬. 엘파이브(L-5) 연락기로 한라산 일대에 전단을 뿌련 투항을 권고하난 하루에도 수십 명씩 떼 지어 귀순자들이 내려와서라."

"바로 그것입쥬. 선무공작은 왜 진작에 쓰지 못했느냐는 말이우다. 처음부터 선무공작을 했으면 인명 피해가 그렇게 많이 나지 않았을 거라 마씸. 폭도도 무섭고 군경도 무서워서 산으로 피난 간 양민들을 폭도로 간주했이니……."

"겔쎄 말이여. 대유격전이란 것이 본디 정치 7에 군사 3인데…… 이건 정치는 쥐뿔도 없고 무작정 군사행동만 했이니…… 창설 일 년도 못된 군대니 오죽할 것고……."

아, 떼죽음당한 마을이 어디 우리 마을뿐이던가. 이 섬 출신이거든 아무라도 붙잡고 물어보라. 필시 그의 가족 중에 누구 한 사람이, 아니면 적어도 사촌까지 중에 누구

rounded up and stripped naked, under the baseless accusation that the girls had joined the Women's Alliance, though the girls didn't even know what the Alliance was about. Sun-i Samch'on was subjected to similar shaming. She was taken to the local police station, where apparently she was stripped at the end of a harsh interrogation about her husband's whereabouts. This was done under the ludicrous pretense of examining her body to determine whether he had visited her the night before. He must have done "it" if he had been with her, and, if so, he must have left the evidence there for them to see, so to speak. I saw one day with my own eyes Sun-i Samch'on being beaten till her head was bleeding, by the Youth Corps police with her own flail, all because she wouldn't tell them her husband's whereabouts.

Besides, the rumor was going around that these guys would sexually assault young women whenever they saw one working alone in the field, making anyone with a grown daughter nervous. Under those circumstances, there was no questioning the wisdom of my grandfather who as a pre-emptive measure chose to marry his own daughter to a Youth-Corps-member-turned-soldier instead of wait-

한 사람이 그 북새통에 죽었다고 말하리라. 군경 전사자 몇 백과 무장 공비 몇 백을 빼고도 오만 명에 이르는 그 막대한 주검은 도대체 무엇인가? 대사를 치르려면 사기그릇 좀 깨지게 마련이라는 속담은 이 경우에도 적용되는가. 아니다. 어디 그게 사기그릇 좀 깨진 정도냐. 아, 멀리 육지에서 바다 건너와 그 자신 적잖은 희생을 치러가면서 폭동을 진압해 준 장본인들에게 오히려 원한을 품어야 하다니, 이 무슨 해괴한 인연인가.

그러나 누가 뭐래도 그건 명백한 죄악이었다. 그런데도 그 죄악은 삼십 년 동안 여태 단 한 번도 고발되어 본 적이 없었다. 도대체가 그건 엄두도 안 나는 일이었다. 왜냐하면 당시의 군 지휘관이나 경찰 간부가 아직도 권력 주변에 머문 채 떨어져 나가지 않았으리라고 섬사람들은 믿고 있기 때문이었다. 선불리 들고 나왔다간 빨갱이로 몰릴 것이 두려웠다. 고발할 용기는커녕 합동 위령제 한번 떳떳이 지낼 뱃심조차 없었다. 하도 무섭게 당했던 그들인지라 지레 겁을 먹고 있는 것이었다. 그렇다. 그들이 원하는 것은 결코 고발이나 보복이 아니었다. 다만 합동 위령제를 한번 떳떳하게 올리고 위령비를 세워 억울한 죽음들을 진혼하자는 것이었다. 그들은 가해자가 쉬쉬해서 삼

ing for her to be raped. At the youthful age of twenty, my inexperienced uncle-to-be fell for Grandfather's clever sweet talk and ended up marrying my aunt, who was two years older.

Anyhow, such a calculated marriage was common in families with escapees. These marriages almost invariably broke down when regiments rotated off the island to the mainland, leaving in their wake children who grew up in sorrow without fathers. Grandfather's careful search for the right person might have paid off, though. Uncle came back to the island for his wife's family after the truce. And he has lived in the area for the last thirty years as an adopted son. How reckless it was for him, given his personal history, to abruptly switch back to the Northern dialect! There was a momentary silence, perhaps because this sudden reversion to his native vernacular reminded the others, as well, of the past that was giving me flashbacks.

The stinging smell of burning dry pine branches came floating across the wooden floor of the entryway, indicating that the rice for the altar was already cooking. We could hear muffled voices in the back alleyways. People must be going to the next house after finishing the service for the first household.

십 년 동안 각자의 어두운 가슴속에서만 갇힌 채 한 번도 떳떳하게 햇빛을 못 본 원혼들이 해코지할까 봐 두려웠다.

선달 열여드레 그날 해질녘이 다 되어서 군인들이 두 대의 스리쿼터에 분승해서 떠난 다음에도 마을 사람들은 그대로 운동장에 남아 있었다. 그들은 조회대 뒤 우익 가족이 있는 데로 몰려 살아남은 가족끼리 서로 붙안고서 마을에서 들려오는 타 죽는 소 울음보다 더 질긴 울음을 입에 물고 있었다. 내 입에서도 겁먹은 울음은 그치지 않았다. 땅거미가 내리기 시작한 운동장의 진창흙은 함부로 내달린 스리쿼터 바퀴 자죽으로 여기저기 무섭게 패어 있고, 벗겨진 만월표 고무신짝들이 수없이 널려 있었다. 그 위로 불타는 마을의 불빛이 밀려와 땅거죽이 붉게 물들었다. 교실 창이 이내 벌게졌다. 그러나 마을 사람들은 하늘 가득히 붉은 노을처럼 번져 가는 불기운에 압도되어 더욱 서럽게 곡성을 올릴 뿐 누구 하나 울타리께로 가서 불타는 마을을 직접 내려다보려는 사람은 없었다.

날이 어두워짐에 따라 마을을 태우는 불빛은 어둠을 사르며 점점 사방으로 퍼져 나갔다. 이것이 일시적으로 확 붉었다가 꺼져 버리는 저녁놀이라면 얼마나 좋을까? 그러나 불빛은 오히려 어두워질수록 더욱더 큼직하게 군림하

Uncle continued to speak with his Northern accent, unaware that it was offensive to the others.

"Islanders still harbor bad feelings about the Youth Corps, I know, but think about it, nephews, why do you suppose the Youth Corps members left their families in the North and came to the South? Nonstop torment by commies forced us to cross the 38th parallel. For us, the commies were the ultimate enemy. What, if not anti-communism, was the reason for the existence of the Youth Corps? We landed in droves on the island in LSTs to establish a frontline against communism because this island was under the rule of the Southern Workers Party. As it turned out, the police and the military were in complete disarray when we joined them. Military discipline was lax and the army was teeming with Southern Workers Party commies. No local military outfit in South Korea was different in that respect, but this island was notorious for an extreme situation. The commanding officer of the regional regiment that consisted mainly of local youths was assassinated, while over a hundred soldiers mutinied and fled to the mountain to join the communist guerillas... We, the Northwest Youth Corps members, filled the vacuum left by over a hundred

여 갔다. 낮게 드리운 구름 떼는 불빛에 물들어 붉은 내장처럼 꿈틀거리고, 바다는 멀리 달려도섬까지 불빛이 벌겋게 번져 나가 마치 들불이 타오르는 형국이었다. 운동장에 모인 사람들의 얼굴에도 더러운 피에 얼룩진 듯 불그림자가 너울거렸다. 마을 쪽에서는 집집마다 불붙은 고방의 쌀독들이 펑펑 터지는 소리가 계속 들려왔다.

할아버지 때문에 안절부절 못하던 큰아버지는 군인들이 마을에서 완전히 철수했다 싶자 변소 가는 척하고 몰래 학교를 빠져나갔다. 할아버지는 며칠 전 남의 집 소뿔에 찔린 허벅지 상처 때문에 기동 못하고 집에 남아 있었던 것이다. 큰아버지는 한참 후에야 맥없이 돌아왔는데 그의 축 늘어진 적삼 소매에서는 연기 냄새가 지독하게 났다. 할머니가 먼저 울음을 터뜨리고 우리도 따라 울었다. 할아버지는 짐작대로 총 맞고 죽어 있었다. 그래도 다행스러운 것은 시신에 화기가 미치지 않은 것이다. 할아버지는 아픈 몸을 이끌고 문짝들을 떼어 텃밭으로 내던지고 난 다음 마지막으로 병풍을 들고 나오다가 감나무 밑에서 총을 맞은 모양이었다.

그날 밤 사람들은 한기를 피해 모두 한 교실로 몰려 들어가 서로 붙안고 밤을 지새웠는데, 밤중에 우리들은 두

deserters. So, from the very start, we were terribly prejudiced against the people of this island. Was it only the Northwest Youth Corps that had a low opinion of islanders? No, it was everyone. It was the same with the locally based outfit from the mainland that came in later to replace our unit. In fact, few on the mainland would have hesitated to consider the entire population of this island communist. The April 3 Riot erupted on the island, sabotage of the May 10 election made the island the only place in South Korea where the election was aborted, the military suffered a mutiny, and it was in the midst of all this turmoil..."

At this point, Older Uncle turned his head away from Uncle with a groan. His eyebrows, wiggling like a pair of caterpillars, indicated that he was exceedingly irritated Uncle stopped with a startled look, probably when he caught himself speaking the Northern dialect. Both Older Tangsuk and Younger Tangsuk were just puffing away at their cigarettes with a sour look on their faces. There was a moment of uncomfortable silence. The usually agreeable Uncle promptly returned to island vernacular to continue his talk.

"Older Brother, in no way am I saying that all was

번 호되게 놀랐었다. 한 번은 마을에서 대밭이 타면서 마구 터지는 폭죽 소리를 총소리로 잘못 알고 놀랐고, 또 한 번은 죽은 줄만 알았던 순이삼촌이 살아 돌아와 밖에서 유리창을 두드렸을 때였다. 삼촌은 밤이 이슥해진 그때까지 시체 무더기 속에 파묻혀 까무러쳐 있었던 것이다. 교실 안에 들어선 당신은 이상하게도 사람들에게 접근하려 들지 않았다. 길수 형이 가서 소매를 잡고 끌어도 막무가내로 뿌리치고 저만치 홀로 떨어져 웅크리고 있었다. 다른 사람들처럼 울지도 않았다. 두 아이를 잃고도 울음이 나오지 않은 것은 공포로 완전히 오관이 봉쇄되어 버린 때문이 아니었을까? 아마 울음은 공포가 물러가는 며칠 후에야 둑이 터지듯 밀려나올 것이었다.

불은 이튿날 아침까지 탔다. 밤새 울음으로 탈진했던 사람들이 날이 새자 아연 활기를 띠었다. 해가 채 떠오르기도 전인데 우리들은 마을로 한꺼번에 몰려갔다. 갯바람에 밀려오는 자욱한 연기 때문에 맞바로 들어갈 수 없어서 멀찍이 바닷가로 우회해서 마을로 들어갔다. 사람들의 눈은, 밤새 뜬눈으로 새우며 운데다 독한 연기를 쐬어서 토끼눈처럼 빨개 있었다. 아니, 살려고 눈이 벌게 있었다는 표현이 더 옳으리라. 불타고 있는 집이 아직도 많아서

well with the Northwest Youth Corps. The Northwest Youth Corps certainly deserves blame for their real wrongdoings. At the same time, it wasn't just the Northwest Youth Corps that thought ill of the inhabitants of this island. Every mainlander shared the same opinion, you know. This misconception was on top of the condescending prejudice that mainlanders already had against islanders... Oh, well."

"You're right. The whole island was taken over by mainlanders back then," Older Tangsuk added, with disgust.

"At that time, the chief of the Hamdŏk police was a native of the island. Even after he told his men emphatically not to execute escapees without orders, those mainlanders looked down on him as a Jeju native, so they just fired away indiscriminately."

Younger Tangsuk waved his hand, expressing his own disagreement.

"Do you really believe that Captain Pak in fact gave such an order? I would wager that he came up with that lame excuse to minimize his own responsibility for killing innocent people."

Cousin Hyŏn-mo seconded Younger Tangsuk. "To the contrary, from what I've heard, Captain Pak was

사람들은 불 꺼진 해변 쪽에 하얗게 몰렸다. 네 집, 내 집이 따로 없었다. 불타버린 집터 아무 데나 들어가 타다 남은 좁쌀, 고구마를 퍼담았다. 고구마 중에도 탄 숯같이 되어 버린 것도 있었지만 먹기 좋게 익은 것도 있어서 사람들은 그것으로 전날 점심과 저녁을 거른 고픈 배를 달랬다. 타 죽은 소, 돼지도 각을 내어 나누어 가졌다.

이렇게 사람마다 등짐 하나씩 만들어 지고 함덕으로 소개하였다. 밤새 울음으로 탈진했던 사람들이 어디서 그런 기운이 났을까? 모두가 보통 때 두 배나 되는 짐을 지어 날랐다. 순이삼촌은 멱서리 하나를 지고도 부족했던지 몸뻬 가랑이에다 탄 좁쌀을 채워 넣어 가지고 함덕까지 시오리 길을 걸어갔던 것이었다. 수용소 시설도 없이 그냥 함덕에 내팽개쳐진 우리 부락 사람들은 우선 잠잘 곳이 문제였다. 용케 빈방이나 온 가족이 다 떠나 버린 도피자 집이 얻어걸린 경우는 다행이었지만, 그렇지 못한 식구들은 말 방앗간이나 남의 집 헛간, 외양간을 빌려 써야만 했다. 하기는 빈방을 구한 사람도 이불 없기는 매한가지라 방에다 보릿짚을 잔뜩 넣고 살았으니 헛간이나 외양간과 별로 다를 게 없었다.

도피자 가족들은 함덕국민학교에 수용되어 취조를 받

even more brutal than the Northwest Youth Corps throughout the whole event."

Uncle picked up on this again.

"That's a plausible scenario. There were some island natives in the police force who were eager to outdo the Northwest Youth Corps by taking even more extreme actions so they wouldn't be accused of being commies themselves by the NYC."

"No, that wasn't the case. The way I heard it from In-su's father who was arrested and freed after interrogation, Captain Pak secretly released several escapees in his custody. It was the mainlanders under him who were vicious."

About two years after the event, Captain Pak came to the village, only to be greeted with hostility. The young man of the house with persimmon trees, who happened to be home on leave but still wearing his military uniform, swung a long stick at Captain Pak, crying out, "Bring back my dead father and my dead brother, you human butcher, you wretched butcher!" That young man, In-gu, was a marine, who joined the military the same day Cousin Hyŏn-mo did.

It was around that time that the combat command headquarters, belatedly remorseful about scorched

고 닷새 만에 풀려나왔는데 순이삼촌도 그중에 끼여 있었다. 그 닷새 동안 할머니 심부름으로 길수 형과 내가 번갈아 가며 차좁쌀 주먹밥을 매일 한 덩어리씩 차입해 주었다. 마지막 날엔 내가 주먹밥을 가지고 가다가 도중에 풀려나오는 순이삼촌을 만났는데 그 몰골은 차마 끔찍한 것이었다. 비녀가 빠져나가 쪽이 풀리고 진흙으로 뒤발한 검정 몸뻬에다 발은 맨발이었는데, 길가 돌담을 짚고 간신히 발짝을 떼며 허위허위 걸어오고 있었다.

삼촌은 서울 우리 집에 있을 적에 궂은날이면 허리뼈가 쑤셔 뜨거운 장판에 지져대곤 했는데, 생각하면 그게 다 그때 얻은 골병임이 틀림없었다.

함덕으로 온 지 두 달도 못되어 양식이 떨어진 피난민들은 들나물과 갯가의 파래나 톳을 삶아 멸치젓 국물에 찍어 먹으면서 간신히 두 달을 버텼는데 그제야 소개령이 해제되어 향리로 돌아갈 수 있었다.

부락민들이 마을에 돌아와서 맨 먼저 한 일은 시체를 처리하는 일이었다. 일주 도로변의 순이삼촌네 밭을 비롯한 네 개의 옴팡밭에 늘비하게 널려진 시체를 제각기 찾아다가 토롱을 만들어 가매장했다. 석 달 가까이 방치되었던 시체들이라 까마귀밥이 되고 풍우에 썩어 흐물흐물

earth tactics, introduced pacification operations and managed to coax a fairly large number of escapees out of the caves. Cousin Hyŏn-mo was one of them. In response to the enlistment efforts following the timely outbreak of the Korean War, ex-escapee defectors fell over themselves volunteering for the South Korean military. There could have been no better opportunity to disprove their unfounded reputation as commies. That was how they escaped this loathsome homeland where they were at risk of being slaughtered like dogs at any moment if they stayed behind. As it turned out, Cousin Hyŏn-mo had joined the very third-year class of marines that would later take part in the Inch'ŏn landing during the Korean War. Thus the famed early marines, dubbed "ghost-busters" for their fearlessness, were principally thirty thousand young men from Jeju Island. Where did their valor come from? Was it overcompensation? Having narrowly escaped death several times after being unfairly labelled communists, they must have been eager to disprove that stigma by demonstrating their anti-communist ferocity. But that wasn't all. Underlying that valor may have been a deep-seated desire for retribution, a desire to visit upon the communist northerners the

문드러져 탈골되었으니, 누구의 시체인지 알아내기가 쉽지 않았다. 겨우 옷가지를 보고 구별했는데 동동네 누구는 제 아버지 시신을 찾아 놓고 지고 갈 지게를 가지러 간 사이에 다른 사람이 잘못 알고 가져가 버린 일도 있었다. 애어머니들은 대개 제 자식의 몸 위에 엎어져 죽어 있었는데 그건 죽는 순간에도 몸으로 총알을 막아 자식을 보호해 보려는 처절한 몸짓이었다.

그럭저럭 시체를 가매장하고 나서 밭에 나가 보리를 거둬들였는데, 거둬들일 시기를 놓친 뒤라 대궁이 썩은 보리들이 온 밭에 늘비하게 쓰러져 몽창몽창 썩고 있었다. 썩어 가는 보리 이삭들은 퍼렇게 싹이 트고 들쥐들이 마구 설쳐댔다. 게다가 난리 때문에 한 번도 김을 못 매어 범이 새끼 치게 잡초가 무성했으니 그해 보리 농사란 게 한 집에 멱서리로 하나가 고작이었다.

그다음에 급히 서둘러 한 일은 움막 짓는 일이었다. 들에서 소나무와 억새를 베어다가 하루 이틀 새에 움막을 세웠다. 칡덩굴로 서까래를 얽어매고 지붕도 벽도 억새를 엮어 둘러쳤다. 게다가 이불과 요를 태워 먹고 없어 보릿짚을 잔뜩 움막 속에 처넣었으니 그건 영락없이 돼지우리였다. 집 말고도 돼지와 똑같은 게 하나 더 있었는데 그건

atrocities of the NYC northerners. The ferocity, celebrated in the history of war, that was displayed by island youths during the Korean War only attests to the profound error of the one-dimensional thinking that once prevailed in the military and police force: the entire population of the island was to be considered communist and killed off, no questions asked. These thoughts stirred an anger pent up deep inside me. I managed to suppress the urge to humiliate Uncle for surreptitiously defending the Northwest Youth Corps. Even so, my comments were sharp.

"Dear Uncle, how many among the three hundred thousand islanders of that time do you suppose were actually commies?"

"Let me see, probably not a whole lot if you leave out about ten thousand unarmed red guerrillas. About three hundred armed guerrillas?"

This ticked me off so much that I lost control.

"What in the world do you mean by unarmed red guerrillas? How can you call unarmed people red guerrillas? They were refugees who, after their mid-mountain villages were scorched, were driven out of their homes into hiding out in the caves scattered in the shadow of Mt. Halla."

Uncle turned toward me as if recoiling in surprise

똥이었다. 양식이 모자라 돼지 사료로 쓰는 밀기울로 범벅해 먹고 파래밥, 톳밥을 해 먹었으니 돼지 똥과 사람 똥이 구별될 리가 없었다.

밀기울 밥도 양껏 먹어 본 적이 없었다. 작은 놋쇠 양푼 하나에 밥을 펴 놓고 네 식구가 둘러앉으면 밥 위에다 숟갈로 금을 그어 제 몫을 표시해 놓고 먹었다. 달려도섬 건너편 갈치밭에 배를 띄우면 그래도 국거리로 살찐 갈치가 꽤 잡힐 텐데, 곧 시작된 성 쌓는 일 때문에 주낙질은 물론 잠녀의 물질도 일체 허락되지 않았다.

부락민들은 순경들의 감독을 받으며 아침부터 저녁까지 한눈팔 새 없이 허기진 배를 안고 성을 쌓지 않으면 안 되었다. 말하자면 전략촌 건설이었다. 불탄 집터의 울담도 허물고 밭담도 허물어다가 성을 쌓았다. 그것도 모자라 묘지를 두른 산담까지 허물어다 날랐다. 순이삼촌도 임신한 몸으로 돌을 져 날랐다.

남정들이 출정해 버린 부락에 남은 건 노인과 아녀자들뿐이라 그 역사는 거의 두 달 가까이나 걸렸다. 전략촌을 두 바퀴 두르는 겹성이었다. 두 성 사이에는 실거리나무, 엄나무 따위 가시 많은 나무를 베어다 넣었다. 길수 형과 나 같은 어린애도 동원된 그 일은 참으로 고되었다. 우선

at my counterargument.

"I think Nephew from Seoul is right about that. I am an eyewitness to that. During an operation in the meadowland, we heard a baby crying. We combed the thick bushes to find a cave in which over twenty unarmed guerillas were hiding."

"Again, they were not unarmed guerillas but refugees."

I firmly corrected Uncle's language a second time.

"That's right. I misspoke again. In those days, anyone who went up the mountain was categorically considered a violent rebel. Anyhow, those in the cave were in terrible shape, beyond description. Starvation had reduced them to skin and bone, they were shivering in a single layer of wet cotton clothes in the dead of winter, and some had already lost toes to frostbite. As so-called unarmed red guerrillas were discovered in such miserable conditions in the caves, the authorities changed their mind in due course and launched appeasement operations, setting up rehabilitation centers stocked with relief supplies. Across the Mt. Halla region, L-5 liaison aircraft dropped flyers urging surrender, leading dozens of defectors to come down in droves each day."

배가 고파 견딜 수 없었다. 허기진 뱃심으로 돌덩이를 들다가 힘에 부쳐 놓치는 바람에 발등을 찍히는 사람들도 많았다. 겨우 성이 완성되자 낮이나마 주낙질과 물질이 허락되었다. 밤이 되면 성문이 닫혀 사람들은 일절 성밖 출입이 금지되고 순번제로 초소막 지키러 나가지 않으면 안 되었다.

국민학교 삼사 학년에서 일 년째 쉬고 있던 나와 길수형도 대창을 하나씩 들고 막을 지키러 나가곤 했다. 순이 삼촌도 만삭의 몸인데도 우리 초소에 대창 들고 막 지키러 나왔다. 사건 날의 그 무서운 공포를 겪었는데도 아기는 떨어지지 않고 살아 있었던 것이다. 사건 날 오누이를 한꺼번에 잃은 삼촌에게는 뱃속의 아기가 유일한 씨앗이었다.

어려운 시절에 아기를 가진 삼촌은 먹을 것을 구하느라고 그야말로 눈이 벌게 있었다. 만삭의 몸이라 물질은 못하고 하루 종일 땡볕에 갯가를 기어 다니며 굴, 성게를 까먹고, 게, 보말(갯우렁이) 따위를 잡았다. 밤에 초소막에 나올 때는 보말 삶은 것 한 채롱 가득 담아 가지고 와서는 우리에게 먹어 보라는 말 한마디 없이 밤새도록 혼자서 걸귀처럼 까먹어대곤 했다. 여자가 아기를 배면 사정없이

"That's exactly what I'm saying. Why didn't they introduce pacification policies sooner? If they had, we would have suffered far fewer human casualties. Instead, those innocent people who took refuge in the caves in fear of both the violent mob and the military and police were condemned as violent rebels..."

"I'm with you on that. Essentially, a guerrilla war should be fought 70 percent politically and 30 percent militarily... In this case, however, there was no politics, only military actions... by a military that wasn't even one year old yet, on top of that..."

Alas, it wasn't just our village that suffered a massacre. Ask anyone from this island that you come across. They'll tell you that a member of their family, or at least someone within their extended family, including first cousins, died during the mayhem. What's the point of massacring as many as fifty thousand people, in addition to several hundred military and police and hundreds of armed guerrillas? Is the old saying that you can't accomplish anything big without breaking some china adequate in this situation? In no way was this massacre equivalent to some broken china. What a bizarre twist of fate for islanders to harbor a grudge toward the very

먹어댄다는 걸 몰랐던 나는 순이삼촌이 걸신들려 실성하지 않았나 생각할 지경이었다.

이런 전략촌 생활은 거의 일 년 넘게 계속되었지만 그동안 한 번도 공비의 습격을 당한 적이 없었다. 한번은 밤중에 성문께에서 무언가 부스럭거리는 소리가 나서 모두 혼비백산한 적이 있었지만, 그건 나중에 알고 보니 낮에 들에서 놓친 누구 집 소가 밤에 제 발로 성까지 걸어와서 부스럭거리고 있었던 것이었다. 결국 해안 지방의 축성은 과잉 조처라는 게 판명된 셈이었다. 이미 몇십 명으로 전력이 크게 줄어든 입산 폭도들은 해안 지방을 약탈할 능력이 전혀 없었다.

부락민들은 일 년이 넘도록 한 번도 써먹어 본 일이 없는 무용지물의 성을 다시 허물고 제각기 제 집터로 돌아갔다. 성을 허문 돌을 날라다가 다시 울담과 벽을 쌓고 새로 집을 지었다. 집이라고 해야 방 하나에 부엌 딸린 두 칸짜리 함바집이었다. 못이 없어서 대신 굵은 철사를 잘라 썼으니 오죽한 집이었을까? 순이삼촌도 우리 큰집에서 몸을 풀고 큰아버지의 도움을 받아 불탄 집터에다 조그만 오두막집을 지어 올렸다. 그러나 일가족이 전부 몰살되어 집을 세우지 못한 채 그대로 방치된 집터도 더러 있었다.

people who crossed the sea from the mainland to quell a violent riot, risking their own lives.

Still, it was clearly a crime no matter how you look at it. And after thirty years, the crime has yet to be reported. In fact, just the thought of raising the issue seems too daunting, since islanders believed that the commanders and leaders of the military and the police force were still active and hanging around the center of power. If they raised the question tactlessly and prematurely, they feared they would be accused of being communists. Far from courageously lodging a complaint, they didn't even have the guts to give the victims a dignified group service. Having been subjected to such extreme terror, they were too fearful. Actually, what they wanted wasn't criminal prosecution or revenge. All they wanted was a dignified public joint memorial service under a monument to pacify the spirits of those unjustifiably killed. They were afraid that those grieving spirits, imprisoned in the dark corners of their hearts and never seeing the light of day, might take their revenge.

Near dusk on that day, December 18, even after the soldiers had left in their small trucks, villagers remained in the schoolyard. The survivors huddled

그 무렵 내 또래 아이들은 사람 죽은 일주 도로변의 옴팡밭에서 탄피를 주워다 화약총을 만들기가 유행이었다. 아이들은 이제 옴팡밭의 비극을 까맣게 잊고 사람 죽인 탄피를 주워 모았다. 그렇다. 무럭무럭 자라는 데 도움 안 되는 것은 무엇이든 편리하게 잊어버리는 게 아이들의 특성이 아닌가. 그러나 어른들은 도무지 잊을 수 없었다. 아이들이 장난으로 팡팡 쏘아대는 화약총 소리에도 매번 가슴이 철렁 내려앉는 그들이었다. 어떤 아이는 어디서 났는지 불에 타서 엿가락처럼 휘어진 총신만 남은 구구식 총을 끌고 다니다가 제 아버지한테 얻어맞고 빼앗겼는데, 총의 그 푸르딩딩한 탄 쇠빛은 꼭 죽은 피 빛깔을 연상시켜 주었다.

그러나 그 누구도 순이삼촌만큼 후유증이 깊은 사람은 없었으리라. 순이삼촌네 그 옴팡진 돌짝밭에는 끝까지 찾아가지 않는 시체가 둘 있었는데 큰아버지의 손을 빌려 치운 다음에야 고구마를 갈았다. 그해 고구마 농사는 풍작이었다. 송장 거름을 먹은 고구마는 목침덩어리만큼 큼직큼직했다.

더운 여름날 당신은 그 고구마 밭에 아기구덕을 지고 가 김을 매었다. 옴팡진 밭이라 바람이 넘나들지 않았다.

together with the right-wing families behind the podium, holding each other tight. The cries that clung to their lips were tougher than the howls of the cows dying in the fire. A terrified cry kept spilling out of my own mouth too. The muddy schoolyard where dusk was starting to set in was violently scarred in places with the tracks of wheels that had skidded around recklessly, and unclaimed Full Moon brand rubber shoes were scattered everywhere. Across it all rushed waves of glowing light from the burning village, drenching the leathery ground in red. The windowpanes of the classrooms turned crimson in no time. Overwhelmed by the power of the fire that was spreading through the entire sky like a scarlet sunset, the surviving villagers intensified their heart-wrenching wail, but none of them even attempted to clamber over the wall and survey the burning village.

As night fell, the glow from the flaming village consumed the darkness and spread in all directions. How we wished it was just a sunset that flares up and fades away. The glow only loomed larger and more domineering as the night got deeper. Hordes of low-lying clouds absorbed the glow and wriggled like red intestines. With the red glow of the fire

고구마 잎줄기는 후줄근하게 늘어진 채 꼼짝도 하지 않았다. 바람 한 점 없는 대낮, 사위는 언제나 조용했다. 두 오누이가 묻힌 봉분의 뗏장이 더위 먹어 독한 풀냄새를 내뿜었다. 돌담 그늘에는 구덕에 아기가 자고 있었다. 당신은 아기구덕에 까마귀가 날아들까 봐 힐끗힐끗 눈을 주면서 김을 매었다. 이랑을 타고 아기구덕에서 아득히 멀어졌다가 다시 이랑을 타고 돌아오곤 했다. 호미 끝에 때때로 흰 잔뼈가 튕겨 나오고 녹슨 납 탄환이 부딪쳤다. 조용한 대낮일수록 콩 볶는 듯한 총소리의 환청은 자주 일어났다. 눈에 띄는 대로 주워 냈건만 잔뼈와 납 탄환은 삼십 년 동안 끊임없이 출토되었다. 그것들을 밭담 밖의 자갈더미 속에다 묻었다.

그 옴팡밭에 붙박인 인고의 삼십 년, 삼십 년이라면 그럭저럭 잊고 지낼 만한 세월이건만 순이삼촌은 그렇지를 못했다. 흰 뼈와 총알이 출토되는 그 옴팡밭에 발이 묶여 도무지 벗어날 수가 없었다. 당신이 딸네 모르게 서울 우리 집에 올라온 것도 당신을 붙잡고 놓지 않는 그 옴팡밭을 팽개쳐 보려는 마지막 안간힘이 아니었을까?

그러나 오누이가 묻혀 있는 그 옴팡밭은 당신의 숙명이었다. 깊은 소 물귀신에게 채여 가듯 당신은 머리끄덩이

stretching all the way up to Tallyŏ Island, the sea looked like a prairie in flames. The shadows of the flames, which resembled dirty blood stains, danced on the faces of the people congregated in the schoolyard. We could hear the incessant popping sound of rice pots bursting in burning pantry rooms coming from the direction of the village.

Thinking of Grandfather, Older Uncle slipped out of the schoolyard on the pretext of relieving himself as soon as he was certain that the soldiers had completely withdrawn from the village. Grandfather had to be left behind at home because he was bedridden after a neighbor's cow had stabbed him in the thigh with its horns some days earlier. Older Uncle came back after a while, dejected, the limp sleeves of his jacket saturated with the strong stench of smoke. Grandmother burst into tears and we followed the suit. Grandfather had been shot dead, as expected. The one bright spot in this misfortune was that his body had not been touched by fire. Apparently, he dragged his ailing body and managed to take the doors off their hinges, throw them into the vegetable garden, and, as his last act, was carrying a folding screen out of the house when he was shot under the persimmon tree.

를 잡혀 다시 그 밭으로 끌리어갔다. 그렇다. 그 죽음은 한 달 전의 죽음이 아니라 이미 삼십 년 전의 해묵은 죽음이었다. 당신은 그때 이미 죽은 사람이었다. 다만 삼십 년 전 그 옴팡밭에서 구구식 총구에서 나간 총알이 삼십 년의 우여곡절한 유예를 보내고 오늘에야 당신의 가슴 한복판을 꿰뚫었을 뿐이었다.

이렇게 생각을 마무리 짓고 나자 나는 문득 담배 피우고 싶은 충동이 조바심치듯 일어났다. 좌중은 어느 틈에 나만 빼놓고 농사 얘기로 동아리져 있었다.

"올해는 제발 작년모냥 감저 시세가 폭락하지 말았이면 좋을로고…… 빌어먹을, 그눔의 가을장마는 뜬금없이 터져 가지고는 썰어 말리던 감저에 곰팽이 피어 부렀이니……."

나는 밖으로 나와 마당귀에 있는 조짚가리에 등을 기대고 담배를 피워 물었다. 마당에 얇게 깔린 싸락눈이 바람에 이리저리 쏠리고 있었다. 음력 열여드레 달은 구름 속에 가려 있었지만 주위는 희끄무레 밝았다. 고샅길로 지나가는 사람들의 기척이 들려왔다. 아마 두어 집째 제사를 끝내고 마지막 집으로 옮아가는 사람들이리라.

『순이삼촌』, 창비, 2006(1978)

That night, the survivors huddled together in one of the classrooms to escape the cold and stayed up all night cuddling one another. We had two terrible scares. One was the wild popping sound of exploding bamboo trees in the burning bamboo grove near the village, which we mistook for gunfire. The other was when Sun-i Samch'on came back from the dead and knocked on the window. She had been unconscious, buried under dead bodies until late at night. Strangely, she wouldn't come near the others when she entered the classroom. After spurning Cousin Kil-su who was tugging her by the sleeve, she kept her distance and curled up alone. She didn't weep like the rest. Probably terror had completely shut down all her senses, since even the loss of her two children failed to make her cry. Only after days had gone by and the terror subsided did her wailing come like waves of water breaking through a levee.

The fire raged on till the next morning. People who had cried themselves to exhaustion seemed to be oddly revived by the dawn. Before the sun rose, we rushed to the village together. The thick smoke, carried by the sea breeze, forced us to take a long detour along the shoreline. Everyone's eyes were as red as a rabbit's from exposure to the toxic smoke as well as staying up all night weeping. Or, more accurately put, their eyes were bloodshot facing the inevitable desperate struggle for survival. Avoiding the several houses still aflame, villagers flocked along the shore like a white blanket covering the area where the fire had run its course. No one cared which house belonged to whom. We entered any lots where the buildings had burned and collected cracked rice and sweet potatoes that survived the firestorm. While some sweet potatoes were completely charred, others were roasted just enough to be edible, and we filled our empty stomachs with them, having had no food since the day before. Cows and pigs, burnt to death, were hacked up and shared.

All of us carrying bundles on our backs, we were evacuated to Hamdŏk. It was astonishing to see people exhausted from crying all night have such energy. All of us were carrying twice as much as we normally could. Sun-i Samch'on walked an hour and a half to Hamdŏk with the legs of her baggy pants filled with half-burnt split rice, as if a stuffed straw bag on her back wasn't enough. Dumped in Hamdŏk with no accommodations, people from our village had to scramble to find a place to sleep for the night. Some were lucky to find an extra room or even an empty house left behind by an escapee family, but others had to settle in a horse mill, or someone's tool shack or cattle barn. Even when rooms were available, they were hardly better than huts and barns as they came bare without mattresses or blankets and had to be furnished with barley straw instead.

Families of escapees were released after five days of detention and interrogation in the Hamdŏk Elementary School building, and Sun-i Samch'on was among them. For those five days, Grandmother had Cousin Kil-su and me take turns delivering daily a fist-sized ball of split extra-sticky sweet rice to her in detention. On the last day, on my way to bring her a rice ball, I ran into her as she had just been released. It was the most shocking sight imaginable. Her hair, which was usually twisted and rolled into a bun, was completely undone since she was missing her hairpin. Her baggy black pants covered with mud, and her feet shoeless, she was walking in my direction, barely able to put one foot in front of the other while leaning on the stone wall along the road.

On rainy days during her stay with us in Seoul, Samch'on would often lie down to press her aching back against the heated floor for a massage. Looking back, I have no doubt that her chronic ailment resulted from what she went through in those days.

The food supplies that the refugees brought to Hamdŏk were gone in less than two months, and we were barely surviving on wild vegetables and seaweed, which we cooked and dipped in salty anchovy brine. The evacuation order was lifted in two months and we could finally return to our village.

The first order of business upon our return was taking care of all the bodies. Each and every one of those bodies strewn on the four sunken fields along the loop, including the one that belonged to Sun-i Samch'on, was claimed and temporarily buried in *makeshift shallow graves.* Nearly three months' exposure to scavenging crows and the elements had left the bodies decomposed, flesh falling off the bones, making identification extremely difficult. Clothing was the only clue, and a tenuous one, of who was who. Someone from the eastern part of the village, for instance, found his father's body, only to realize, when he returned with an A-frame rack on which to carry the body, that someone else had mistakenly claimed and removed it from the site. Mothers were often found on top of their children, suggesting that they had desperately attempted to shield them from the bullets with their own bodies at the very moment of their deaths.

After they managed to give the bodies temporary burials, villagers went into the fields to glean barley. Since harvest time had already passed, the bottoms of the stalks were rotten, so the barley had fallen on the ground and was decomposing. Disintegrating barley ears were shooting green sprouts to the delight of restless field mice. Besides, the fields, untended during the disturbance, were overgrown with thick weeds that could have easily provided tigers with cover for a batch of cubs. The barley harvest that year amounted to no more than one straw bag for each household.

The next urgent task the villagers faced was constructing some sort of basic shelter. It took a day or two to cut down the pine trees and purple eulalia growing in the fields to build sheds. Arrowroot vines were used to tie rafters together, while the roof and walls were thatched with interwoven eulalia. Having lost mattresses and blankets in the fire, we lined the sheds with plenty of barley straw and they resembled pig pens when they were finished. Another trait we shared with the pigs was dung. A food shortage left us with few options except a hot porridge of the inner chaff of wheat, ordinarily fed to pigs, and various cooked sea lettuce or laver meals. This diet made it hard to tell pig droppings from human excrement.

Even wheat chaff porridge was never available enough to satisfy our hunger. When four of us as a family would sit around a small copper bowl of porridge, we would draw lines with our spoons to mark our share before digging in. If we had gone out in a fishing boat to the hairtail farm across from Tallyŏ Island we could have had fat hairtails good for gumbo soup. But fishing with a reel and multiple hooks and gathering of seaweed and shellfish by female divers had been banned, because the fortress building project had just begun.

The villagers, under police supervision, were being forced to build fortifications on empty stomachs from dawn till dusk. Walls surrounding burnt-down houses or demarcating patches of field were knocked down and their stones used for the fortress. As if that wasn't enough, the hillside walls that protected graves were knocked down and used for the project as well. Sun-i Samch'on carried rocks on her back despite being pregnant.

The public construction project, carried out mostly by the elderly, women, and children left behind as the men joined the military and shipped out for the war, took nearly two months to complete. It consisted of double walls surrounding the strategic hamlet. The space between the two walls was filled with the branches of trees such as *shilgŏri* and thorny ash Children as young as Cousin Kil-su and I were mobilized for the project though it involved hard labor. Our hunger was the most unbearable thing. Many people suffered injuries to their feet because, weakened by hunger, they frequently lost their grip and dropped heavy rocks on themselves. When the fortress was finally finished, the ban on fishing and diving for seaweed and shellfish was lifted. At night, the fortress gate was closed, locking us inside, and we had to take turns at guard duty.

Cousin Kil-su and I, fourth- and third-graders with no school for that entire year, would go out to guard the post, each armed with a bamboo spear. In spite of her full-term pregnancy, Sun-i Samch'on came out with a bamboo spear for her guard duty too. The baby had survived the terror she had been subjected to that fateful day. Because she had lost both her son and daughter then, the baby inside her was her only hope to save her family bloodline.

Pregnancy in such a lean time left Samch'on absolutely desperate for food. Since she was expecting any moment now, diving was out of the question. Instead, she crawled around the shore of the inlet all day under the scorching sun, preying on oysters and sea cucumbers, and gathering sea snails. When she came out to the post at night, she would bring a basketful of boiled sea snails, which she would pry open and gulp down all through the night, as if possessed by a starving ghost, without offering any to us. Unaware that expecting moms have a seemingly limitless appetite, I was almost convinced that Sun-i Samch'on, overcome by hungry ghouls, had lost her mind.

These living conditions at the strategic hamlet continued for over a year, but we were never attacked by armed guerillas during that time. One time some suspicious noises around the fortress gate scared us out of our wits. It turned out to be a villager's cow that had broken out during the day and walked all the way back to the hamlet from the pasture at night. In the end, the construction of fortresses along the shores proved to be a zealous over-reaction. Armed insurgents in the mountains had already been reduced to a meager force of less than a hundred, with hardly any capability to raid coastal areas.

The villagers returned to the sites of their own houses after tearing down the useless fortress walls that they had never had to use for over a year. Rocks from the demolished fortress were brought back to be used for the walls and fences of their new homes. With only two spaces, a main room and a kitchen, these shacks could hardly be called houses. Needless to say, their quality was below substandard as thick wires had to be cut and used in place of real nails. After giving birth to her child at Uncle's place, Sun-i Samch'on also built a tiny hut with his help on the lot of her burnt-down house. There were also abandoned lots where no new construction replaced scorched houses; these were homes where the entire family had been wiped out.

Around that time, it became a popular pastime for kids my age to make firecrackers out of empty cartridges found in the sunken fields along the loop road where the mass killing took place. Children no longer remembered the tragedy when they were collecting the empty cartridges used to murder people. Isn't one of the qualities of children the convenient failure to remember whatever isn't beneficial to their vigorous development? But adults were unable to get the event out of their mind. The loud bang of the firecrackers the kids were setting off never failed to make the adults' hearts jump. One of the kids got a good spanking from his father for dragging around the warped barrel of a burnt-out '99-style' rifle. His father took it away from him. The bluish singed-metal hue of the rifle reminded me of the color of the shed blood.

No one probably was more profoundly affected by the aftermath of the massacre than Sun-i Samch'on. She was able to plant sweet potatoes in her sunken patch of rocky soil only after the two unclaimed bodies were removed by Uncle's helping hand. That year produced an unusually large crop of sweet potatoes. Nourished by the compost of dead bodies, sweet potatoes grew as big as wooden pillows.

On steamy summer days, she carried her baby in a basket on her back to her sweet potato field, and weeded and dug. Hardly any wind moved in or out of that sunken ground. The potato stems were wilted and motionless. At midday when there was no breeze, there was always total silence from all directions. Distressed from the heat, the grass covering the grave mound where her daughter and son were buried gave off a pungent odor. In the shadow of the stone wall surrounding her patch, her baby was asleep in a basket. While weeding the field, she would frequently glance at the basket to guard against swooping crows. She would follow the furrow to the farthest end from the basket and return along the next furrow. From time to time, small white bones would spring out and rusty lead bullets would clang at the stroke of her hoe. More frequently during the quiet midday, she would have an auditory hallucination of gunfire, like corn popping. Even as she picked out every little piece of bone and lead bullet she encountered, she kept discovering more for the next thirty years. She buried them under the piles of rock outside the wall.

After the harsh, grinding thirty years she spent in bondage to the sunken field, after the thirty years that would be long enough to make most people forget and forgive almost anything, Sun-i Samch'on couldn't move on. She couldn't break away from the past with her feet chained to the sunken patch that was still producing white bones and lead bullets. Coming to live with us in Seoul without letting her daughter know might have been her final forlorn attempt to shake off that sunken patch of land.

Nevertheless, that sunken land where her two children were buried was her destiny. She was snagged and dragged back to the patch by her hair as if lured into a bottomless pond by a water ghost. Her death wasn't a month-old event. It was an old death that had happened thirty years ago. She had been dead ever since. The bullet that left the muzzle of a '99-style' rifle thirty years ago had finally penetrated her heart a month ago, after having slowly traced its tortuous thirty-year trajectory.

When I came to this conclusion, I felt a sudden urge to smoke. I realized that the group had already moved on without me to all-engrossing farming topics.

"I sure hope the market price of potatoes this year won't bottom out like it did last year... Damn it, thanks to the unexpected rainy season in the fall, those potatoes, cut up and spread out for drying, are now growing moldy... "

I stepped outside to light a cigarette with my back

against a stack of millet straw in a corner of the front yard. A thin layer of small, dry snow pellets on the ground was drifting around in the wind. The moon of the eighteenth day of the lunar calendar was obscured by clouds, but there was enough light to discern my surroundings. I could hear people walking down the alley. They must have been on their way to the last house after several rounds of memorial services.

Translated by Lee Jung-hi

해설

Afterword

금기를 넘어, 치유를 향하여

오창은(문학평론가)

제주도는 '신비의 섬'이라고 불리는 낭만적 휴양지다. 최근에는 '제주 올레길'로 인해 '가고 싶은 곳, 걷고 싶은 곳'의 대표적인 명소가 되었다. 하지만 해방 후 제주도가 역사적 상처를 안고 있는 곳이라는 사실은 숨겨져 왔다. 정치권력에 의해 제주도의 역사적 아픔은 수십 년 동안 금기시 되었고, 제주도민들 또한 그 고통을 공개적으로 이야기하지 못했다.

현기영의 「순이삼촌」(1978)은 한 개인이 감당하고 있는 고통의 근원을 추적함으로써, 제주도라는 공동체 전체가 겪은 고통의 뿌리를 들춰낸다. 그 중심에 1948년 4·3 민중항쟁이 있다. 제주 4·3 민중항쟁은 미군정기에 '남한

Beyond Taboo, Toward Healing

Oh Chang-eun (literary critic)

Jeju Island is a romantic resort nicknamed the "Mysterious Island." Recently it has become one of the most desired tourist destinations for walking tours, thanks to the "Jeju Ole Course." By contrast, the fact that Jeju Island has suffered from a trauma inflicted immediately after the liberation of the country has been hidden from public view. Authorities forced Jeju Island's historical trauma to be a taboo subject, and as a result, the island's people could not openly talk about the pain from which they have been suffering for a long time.

Hyun Ki-young "Sun-i Samch'on" (1978) reveals

단독정부 수립'을 반대하는 제주도 남로당 무장대와 경찰 토벌대가 무력 충돌한 사건이다. 이 사건으로 인해 제주도민 삼만 명이 희생되었다고 추정하는데, 이는 전체 제주도민의 십 퍼센트에 해당하는 인원이다. 문제는 이 사건이 2000년 1월 12일, 제주 4·3 특별법이 제정되기 전까지는 진상 조사도 제대로 이뤄지지 않았다는 사실이다.

「순이삼촌」은 '나'가 고향 제주도를 찾아가는 장면으로 시작한다. 화자인 '나'는 팔 년 동안이나 고향인 제주도를 방문하지 못했다. 내가 고향을 회피한 이유는 그곳이 '깊은 우울증과 찌든 가난밖에 남겨 준 것이 없'다는 인식 때문이다. 그렇다면, 깊은 우울증의 근원은 어디인가? 이 소설은 나의 상처(깊은 우울증)를 발견하고, 그것을 가족들과 공유한 후, 치유하는 과정을 다룬 이야기이다. 팔 년 만의 고향 방문은 '조부모 제사'에 꼭 내려와 가족 묘지 매입 문제를 상의하자는 큰아버지의 부름 때문에 이뤄진다.

'나'는 온 가족이 모이는 할아버지 제삿날에 '순이삼촌'이 보이지 않는 사실을 발견한다. 순이삼촌은 서울 '나'의 집에 일 년여 동안 있다 두 달 전에야 제주도로 귀향했다. 그런데 순이삼촌에 그사이에 스스로 목숨을 끊고 만 것이다. 순이삼촌에 대한 죽음을 계기로 할아버지의 제삿날이

the depths of the Jeju community's suffering by tracing an individual's pain to its origin. At the source of his pain lies the 4.3 Uprising in 1948, which occurred after an incident in which the armed youth of the Jeju division of the South Korean Communist Party and the police punitive forces clashed. There were an estimated thirty thousand victims during this uprising, a tenth of Jeju Island's population. Even more painful to the victims and their families is the fact that the truth of this incident could not be investigated until the Jeju 4.3 Special Act passed the legislature on January 12, 2000.

"Sun-i Samch'on" begins with a scene in which the narrator visits his home village on Jeju Island, a place he has not seen for eight years. He has avoided his village because he thinks that it only left him with severe depression and extreme poverty. But what is the origin of his severe depression? The story deals with the narrator's realization of his own trauma (and depression), his sharing it with his family, and their communal healing. The narrator returns to his home village after receiving a call from an uncle who wants him to attend the memorial ceremony for his grandparents and to participate in a discussion on the family burial ground.

기도 한 '음력 선달 열여드레'에 벌어진 사건에 대해 모두 이야기를 나누게 된다.

도대체 '음력 섣달 열여드렛날'에 무슨 일이 발생한 것일까? 이 소설은 순이삼촌의 자살을 계기로 팽팽한 긴장 속에서 1949년에 있었던 '북촌리 대학살 사건'의 진상을 추적해 들어간다. 1948년 4·3 민중항쟁이 있은 이후, 일 년여 만에 발생한 '북촌리 대학살'은 군인들에 의해 주민 오백 명이 살해당한 사건이다. 마을을 소개하라는 명령을 받은 군인들이 주민들을 선별해 무장대로 간주한 후 사살한 것이다. 따라서 할아버지의 제삿날은 단지 할아버지의 죽음만을 기리는 날이 아니라, 온 동네가 제사를 치르며 참혹한 상흔을 기억하는 날인 것이다. 이 응어리는 이야기의 향연으로 조금씩 풀려나간다. 동네의 거의 모든 집들이 제사를 지내는 '음력 섣달 열여드렛날'의 이야기를 통해 '한풀이'가 이뤄진 것이다. 이 한풀이는 다른 측면에서 '내'가 그동안 회피해 왔던 '고향'을 다시 발견하고 껴안는 것이기도 하다.

당시 군경의 입장을 대변하는 고모부(서북청년단 출신)와 피해자 측을 대변하는 가족들의 설전은 핍진하게 사건을 재구성하는 역할을 한다. 역사적 사건에 대한 다양한

On the day of the memorial ceremony, the narrator realizes that Sun-i Samch'on is missing. Sun-i Samch'on had returned to Jeju Island two months after staying in the narrator's house for about a year. It turns out that she committed suicide in the interim. This death triggers a family conversation about a past incident that happened on the eighteenth day of the twelfth lunar month, the day of the memorial ceremony for the narrator's grandfather, in 1949.

What happened on that day? The story suspensefully traces the truth of the Bukchonri Massacre Incident. During this massacre that happened a year after the 4.3 Incident in 1948, soldiers brutally murdered five hundred inhabitants of Bukchonri in order to evacuate the village. Soldiers simply shot and killed five hundred civilians who did not want to leave, categorically classifying them as guerrillas. As a result, the day of the memorial ceremony for the narrator's grand-father is not just a day for remembering him as an individual, but a day in which all villagers simultaneously hold a memorial service for their ancestors and remember their common trauma. Their bitterness is gradually resolved during a feast of storytelling. They relieve their resentment through communal storytelling on the

입장을 보여 줌으로써 사건의 이면을 보다 깊숙이 들춰내고 있는 것이다. 주목할 부분은 '북촌리 대학살'이 '구술(제삿날 이야기)' 형식을 빌어 '문자(소설)'로 기록되고 있다는 사실이다. 구술은 4·3 민중항쟁에 대해 문자로 기록을 남길 수 없는 상황에서, 이야기의 형식으로 기억을 지속하고자 하는 제주도민의 의지가 집약되어 있는 것이다. 이것을 문자언어인 소설로 형상화한 현기영은 '은폐되어 있는 역사적 사건'을 공식화하려는 지식인 작가의 의지 표출이라고 할 수 있다.

이 소설이 흥미로운 지점은 '순이삼촌이라는 개인을 이야기하면서, 실제로는 제주도라는 역사적 경험 공동체의 상처, 그리고 한반도 전체가 겪은 험난한 역사'를 파헤친다는 데 있다. 이 소설에서 북촌리 대학살에서 살아남은 순이삼촌이 평생을 '정신적 상처'에 고통받으며 살아왔다. 군인과 순경은 먼빛으로만 봐도 질겁했고, 극심한 결벽증으로 전전긍긍하는 삶을 살았으며, 환청 증세로 인해 피폐한 삶을 살아야 했다. 순이삼촌의 고통은 단지 개인의 고통이 아니다. 그것은 4·3 사건을 공개적으로 이야기할 수 없는 제주도민의 응어리를 표현한 것이고, 국가 폭력에 대한 극심한 공포심을 표현한 것이기도 하다.

day of a communal memorial ceremony. This is also an occasion for the narrator to rediscover and embrace his home village, which he has been avoiding.

Arguments between one of the narrator's uncles (a member of the Northwest Youth Corps at the time), who represents the perspective of the soldiers and police, and the rest of the family, who represent the victims, reflect conflicting viewpoints about the event, contributing to a deeper and fuller representation of its truth. It is noteworthy that the Bukchonri Massacre Incident is being recorded in written language, but in the form of oral histories (storytelling during the memorial ceremony). These oral histories express the will of the people of Jeju to perpetuate their memories through storytelling when they were not allowed to record the incident in written language. By embodying these oral histories in a written short story, Hyun Ki-young shows the will of an intellectual who intends to bring a hidden historical incident into the arena of public discourse.

This story superbly exposes the trauma of a community that shares the same historical experience, as well as the tumultuous history of the entire Korean

「순이삼촌」이 써진 시기가 1978년이라는 사실에 비춰 볼 때, 현기영은 문학 작품으로 '금기'를 건드린 작가이다. 「순이삼촌」은 '4·3 민중항쟁'과 '북촌리 대학살'을 공개적으로 이야기하지 못하던 시기에 문학 작품으로 '역사적 진실'을 묘파한 문제작이었다. 이 작품을 발표한 후, 현기영은 국가 기관인 합동수사본부에 체포되어 고문을 당했고, 단편집 『순이삼촌』이 금서로 묶이는 필화 사건을 겪었다. 「순이삼촌」이라는 작품을 통해 제주도민의 아픈 응어리를 어루만져 주었던 현기영은 또 다른 국가폭력의 희생양이 되었다. 그런 의미에서 이 작품은 해방기 민중 수난의 기록이면서, 동시에 1970년대 후반의 엄혹한 시대 상황을 증언하는 문제작이다.

peninsula, through the story of an individual named Sun-i Samch'on. A survivor of the Bukchonri Massacre, Sun-i Samch'on suffered from the trauma inflicted on her by this incident for the rest of her life. She was terrified by even glimpsing soldiers and policemen in the distance, and led an extremely nervous life, impoverished and suffering from a pathological fear of germs and auditory hallucinations. Her pain was not simply the pain of an individual. It was also the pain and resentment of the people of Jeju Island, who could not openly discuss the 4.3 Incident. Her pain also expresses the extreme fear, experienced by the people of Jeju, of state violence.

By publishing this story in 1978, Hyun Ki-young dared to challenge the taboo about this subject that had been forced onto society by the state. "Sun-i Samch'on" is a "controversial work" dealing with historical truth through literature at a time when one could not openly speak about the 4.3 Incident or the Bukchonri Massacre Incident. After the publication of this story, Hyun was arrested and tortured by the Joint Investigation Headquarters and his short story collection *Sun-i Samch'on*, containing the title story, was banned. In his attempt to alleviate the painful feelings of the people of Jeju Island, Hyun himself became another victim of state violence. In this sense, his short story is not only a record of the people's suffering after the liberation of Korea, but also a testimony to the harsh political reality in the late 1970's.

비평의 목소리

Critical Acclaim

역사와 작가가 만나는 공간이 작중인물의 개인의식으로 되는 주인공 소설에서 비관과 환상은 필연적이다. 한편 「순이삼촌」의 현기영은 주인공 소설에서는 종합적으로 다루기 힘든 역사적 역장(力場)을 '사건' 속에 펼쳐 놓고 있다. 그에게 1948년의 제주도 양민학살 사건은 한국사의 비극과 개인사적 비극이 구별될 수 없는 현장이다. 현기영의 테마는 역사가 보편적 정의에 의해서 그 진상을 드러내야 한다는 것이다. 그의 주인공은 인물이 아니라 사건이다. 개인적 초월에의 의지가 거대한 역사의 수레바퀴에 부닥쳐 파탄하거나 환상으로 변질할 수밖에 없음이 주인공 소설의 결말이라면 현기영은 바로 그러한 사실의 인

Pessimism and illusion may be inevitable in a first-person narrative in which the author encounters history through the consciousness of the main character. In "Sun-i Samch'on", Hyun Ki-young tackles a very difficult literary task: depicting the historical field of power through a first-person narrative of an incident. For Hyun, the civilian massacres on Jeju Island in 1948 are a space in which historical tragedy is indistinguishably intertwined with personal tragedies... Hyun here argues that history should reveal its truth within the framework of universal justice. The main character in his story is not a person, but an incident. The first-person narrative typi-

식에서 시작한다.

송상일

해방 직후 제주도 4·3 사건을 소재로 이데올로기의 편견과 폭력에 의해 파리 목숨처럼 죽어간 제주도민의 대수난(작가는 당시 25만 인구 중에서 5만가량이 살상당한 것으로 추정한다)을 그린 「순이삼촌」이 던져 준 엄청난 충격은 6·25 당시 커다란 물의를 일으켰던 거창 양민학살 사건과도 비견할 바가 아니다. 불과 몇백 명의 폭도를 색출하기 위해 몇만 명의 무고한 인명이 희생되는 어처구니없는 만행은 어떤 이데올로기적 정당성으로도 도저히 해명될 수 없는 부분이다. 「순이삼촌」이 70년대 선보인 어떤 분단 소재의 작품보다 감동적인 것은 학살 당시의 후유증으로 삼십 년 동안을 피해망상에 시달리다 마침내 비극적인 자살로 마감되는 한 여인의 생애가 그대로 분단의 현재적 단면임을 적나라하게 확인시켜 준 데서 연유한다.

김도연

의문-추적 형식은 어둠 속에 묻혔던 제주도 4·3 항쟁의 실상에 대한 객관적 탐구의 첫걸음인 이 작품의 의의를

cally ends with the collapse of an individual's will to transcend reality or with the transformation of this will into an illusion after the individual's collision with the giant wheel of history. Hyun story begins with this knowledge instead of ending with it.

Song Sang-il

"Sun-i Samch'on" depicts the catastrophic result of ideological prejudice and violence in the case of the suffering of the people of Jeju Island during the 4.3 Incident that occurred soon after the liberation of Korea. Hyun estimates that about 50,000 people out of a population of 250,000 were killed or wounded during this incident, whose shocking scale far exceeds that of the Geochang Civilian Massacre Incident, which received great attention during the Korean War. No ideology can justify such absurd brutality that sacrificed tens of thousands of innocent civilian lives in the name of pursuing a few hundred rebels. "Sun-i Samch'on" stands out, even among stories dealing with problems related to the division of the country, as it successfully represents our collective lives in a divided nation through the description of the life of a single woman who has suffered from paranoia ever since the massacre, and

집약한다. 그러나 어디 4·3 항쟁에만 국한되는 것이겠는가. 그것은 이데올로기적인 금제에 막혀 왜곡 은폐되었던 우리 근현대사의 안쪽에 대한 객관적 탐구를, 나아가서는 금기를 뚫고 진실의 규명에 나아가려는 모든 지향을 추동하는 실천의 형식이다. 「순이삼촌」의 이 의문-추적의 형식은 지난 80년대를 뜨겁게 달구었던 과거 탐구와 금기의 해체 작업을 앞서 이끄는 사상사적 의미를 지닌 것이다.

정호웅

제삿집에 모인 제주 사람들은 1948년에서 1954년까지 수만의 인명을 앗아가며 전개된 끔찍한 사태를 되풀이해서 이야기한다. '하도 들어서 귀에 못이 박인 이야기'를 계속해서 되뇐다. 사람들은 오랜 세월이 흘렀어도 참혹했던 시절의 기억을 결코 잊지 않는다. '오히려 잊힐까 봐 제삿날마다 모여' 당시의 사연들을 이야기하며 '그때 일을 명심해 두는' 것이었다. 제주 사람들은 이야기를 '제사 때마다 귀에 못이 박일 정도로 들었'기에 언제나 그 이야기들이 '머릿속에 무성하게' 살아 움직이고 있었던 것이다. 이렇게 제주 사람들은 제삿날마다 모여서 괴롭고 비참한 기억이지만 잊히지 않도록 명심하여 구전하고 있었다.

eventually commits suicide.

Kim Do-yeon

This story takes the form of solving a mystery, appropriate for our first step towards objectively exploring the truth behind the Jeju 4.3 Uprising. Yet, how could the story's significance be limited to the truth of this one event? The same structure can, in fact, be adopted for all actions that encourage us to pursue the truth despite the barrier of ideological taboo. That "Sun-i Samch'on" is structured as a mystery is a significant event in the history of our thought, because it led to further efforts to break the silence about the past and encourage the pursuit of truth, which intensified in 1980's Korea.

Jung Ho-ung

People on Jeju Island gather for memorial ceremonies and talk over and over again about the horrible incident that cost the lives of tens of thousands of civilians from 1948 to 1954. They keep on talking about this story that "is stuck in their ears because they have heard it too many times." Although many years have passed, they cannot forget the memories of this horrendous past. "On the contrary, in order

'식겟집 문학'(제삿집 담소문학)의 실체는 바로 이런 것이었다. 현기영은 그런 응어리를 터뜨려 분출시킨 것이다. 그러기에 「순이삼촌」은 '식겟집 문학'이 제도권 문학의 형식으로 현현된 증언 문학이며, 아울러 4·3 담론을 구전문학에서 기록문학으로 전환한 소설인 셈이다.

김동윤

not to forget, they gather on the day of the annual memorial ceremony and try to make sure to remember the incident of old" by talking about their individual experiences. As the people of Jeju Island hear the same stories over and over again at the annual memorial ceremony, these stories continue to live on 'vigorously' in their minds. Through this process, the people of Jeju orally hand down their memories—although painful and wretched—every time they conduct a memorial ceremony, so that they won't ever forget them. This is the very essence of siggedjip literature (the literature of memorial ceremony chat). By means of his short story, Hyun Ki-young channels this talk by people on the day of the memorial ceremony. "Sun-i Samch'on" is part of the literature of testimony, i.e. siggedjip literature that enters the world of formal literature, a novel that transforms our discourse on the 4.3 Incident from oral literature into written.

Kim Dong-yun

현기영

작가 현기영은 1941년 제주에서 태어났다. 1948년 4월 3일 제주에서는 도민들이 민중봉기를 일으켜 그중 삼만 명이 군·경찰에 의해 학살당하는 4·3 항쟁이 있었다. 이 사건은 작가 현기영의 인생을 결정짓게 된다. 여덟 살이라는 어린 나이에 수많은 사람이 죽어 가는 것을 목격한 현기영은 그때부터 우울증과 말더듬을 겪게 된다. 어린 시절 그는 우울과 슬픔으로부터 벗어나려는 본능으로 늘 동무들 가운데 끼어 있기를 좋아했다. 마치 자신의 말더듬을 벌충하려는 듯 충동적이고 난폭하게 놀았다. 때문에 하마터면 목숨을 잃을 뻔한 적도 있었다. 그는 자신의 답답한 말더듬으로부터 벗어나고자 책을 소리 내어 읽어 보기도 하고, 혓바닥과 턱 운동을 하기도 했지만 모두 헛수고였다.

유년의 현기영은 자신의 내면에 있는 억압 때문에 권위주의적인 어른들은 비정상적이다 할 정도로 두려워했다. 또한 그들을 증오하는 마음은 마치 간질 발작처럼 문득문득 고개를 쳐들어 그를 사나운 격정으로 휩싸이게 했다. 고등학교 삼 학년 때 그는 두 번의 자살 기도를 하게 된다.

Hyun Ki-young

Hyun Ki-young was born in Jeju in 1941. There was a people's uprising in Jeju Island on April 3rd, 1948, during which about 30,000 people were massacred by the military and police. This incident has had a lasting influence on Hyun's life. After witnessing the massacre as a child, Hyun suffered from depression and a stutter. During his childhood, he always preferred being with his friends, perhaps because he instinctively tried to get away from sadness and depression. Also, perhaps in order to compensate for his stutter, he acted impulsively and harshly, which once caused him almost to lose his life. In order to cure his stutter, he in vain practiced reading books aloud and tried tongue and jaw exercises.

During his childhood, Hyun extremely feared authoritarian adults probably because of the inner suppression from which he was suffering. He was also often overwhelmed by strong hatred towards them. He attempted suicide twice during high school.

All things that oppressed Hyun eventually inevitably

그를 억압하던 것들이 그로 하여금 유신 정권의 폭정 속에서도 제주 4·3 항쟁을 소재로 한 소설을 쓰도록 이끌었다. 그는 1967년 서울대학교 영어교육학과를 졸업하고 중학교 영어 교사 생활을 하면서 소설 창작을 병행한다. 그리고 1975년 《동아일보》에 「아버지」가 당선되면서 등단한다.

그는 1978년 「순이삼촌」을 쓰면서 본격적으로 4·3 항쟁의 아픔을 작품에 담기 시작했다. 이 작품으로 그는 경찰에 끌려가 고문을 당하는 수난을 겪었지만 이 작품은 1970년대 최고의 문제작으로 평가받음으로써 향후 작품 세계를 결정짓는 계기가 되었다. 이어 4·3 사건을 문학적 화두로 삼아 「도령마루의 까마귀」(1979), 「해룡 이야기」(1979), 「길」(1981), 「어떤 생애」(1983), 「아스팔트」(1984) 등의 작품을 잇달아 발표하면서 역사적 수난기에 처한 제주 민중의 삶을 치밀하게 탐색해 '4·3 작가'로 불리게 된다. 이러한 문학적 활동과 함께 제주 4·3 연구소 소장과 제주사회문제협의회 회장 등을 역임하며 꾸준히 4·3 관련 활동을 펼치고 있다.

led him to write stories dealing with the Jeju 4.3 Uprising under the harsh Yushin regime. After he graduated from the College of Education at Seoul National University, majoring in English education, in 1967, he worked as an English teacher, while writing at the same time. He made his literary debut in 1975, as his short story "Father" won the *Dong-A Ilbo* Spring Literary Contest.

Since 1978, when he published *Suni Samch'on*, he began writing about trauma and pain of the 4.3 Uprising. Although Hyun was detained and tortured by the police for this short story, he also became one of the most critically acclaimed authors of the 1970's due to this work. He continued to publish stories related to the 4.3 Uprising including "Crow on Toryong Ridge," (1979) "Story of Haeryong" (1979), "Road" (1981), "A Life" (1983), and "Asphalt" (1984), acquiring the nickname "the 4.3 author" as a writer who explored details of people's lives in Jeju during a period of historical suffering. He has also been actively involved in the movement on the 4.3 Uprising, working as the director of the Jeju 4.3 Institute and the Jeju Council for Social Problems. He served on the board of directors for the Writers Association for National Literature and worked as the President of the Arts Council Korea. He is the recipient of the Manhae Literary Award (1989) and the *Hankook Ilbo* Literary Award (1999).

번역 **이정희** Translated by Lee Jung-hi

전북대학교에서 영어교육학을 전공한 후, 미네소타 주립대학교 신문방송학과에서 석사 학위를(1991), 메사추세츠 주립대학교 커뮤니케이션학과에서 박사 학위(1998)를 받았다. 한인 사회 안팎에서 저널리스트로 일했고, 여성과 초기 이민자들을 위한 비영리 사회단체들과 함께 활동했으며, 현재는 메사추세츠에서 프리랜서로 번역과 통역 일을 하고 있다.

Lee Jung-hi is B.Ed. in English Education at Chŏnbuk National University (1978); M.A. in Mass Communication at University of Minnesota Twin Cities (1991); Ph.D. in Communication Theory at the University of Massachusetts-Amherst (1998); worked for a Korean-American newspaper and other non-profit organizations for women and new immigrants in the Chicago area in 1990 - 1992; has been a freelance translator and interpreter in Central Massachusetts.

감수 **K. E. 더핀** Edited by K. E. Duffin

시인, 화가, 판화가. 하버드 인문대학원 글쓰기 지도 강사를 역임하고, 현재 프리랜서 에디터, 글쓰기 컨설턴트로 활동하고 있다.

K. E. Duffin is a poet, painter and printmaker. She is currently working as a freelance editor and writing consultant as well. She was a writing tutor for the Graduate School of Arts and Sciences, Harvard University.

감수 **전승희** Edited by Jeon Seung-hee

번역문학가, 문학평론가. 하버드대학교 한국학연구소 연구원으로 재직 중이며 바흐친의 『장편소설과 민중언어』, 제인 오스틴의 『오만과 편견』 등을 공역했다.

Jeon Seung-hee is a literary critic and translator. She is currently a fellow at the Korea Institute, Harvard University. Her translations include Mikhail Bakhtin's *Novel and the People's Culture* and Jane Austen's *Pride and Prejudice*.

바이링궐 에디션 한국 대표 소설 003
순이삼촌

2012년 7월 25일 초판 1쇄 발행
2025년 6월 20일 초판 6쇄 발행

지은이 현기영 | **옮긴이** 이정희 | **감수** K. E. 더핀, 전승희
펴낸이 김재범 | **기획위원** 전성태, 정은경, 이경재
디자인 나루기획 | **인쇄·제책** 굿에그커뮤니케이션 | **종이** 한솔PNS
펴낸곳 (주)아시아 | **출판등록** 2006년 1월 27일 제406-2006-000004호
주소 경기도 파주시 회동길 445
전화 031.944.5058 | **팩스** 070.7611.2505 | **전자우편** bookasia@hanmail.net
ISBN 978-89-94006-20-8(set) | 978-89-94006-22-2(04810)
값은 뒤표지에 있습니다.

Bi-lingual Edition Modern Korean Literature 003
Sun-i Samch'on

Written by Hyun Ki-young | **Translated by** Lee Jung-hi
Published by ASIA Publishers
Address 445, Hoedong-gil, Paju-si, Gyeonggi-do, Korea
Tel. (8231).944.5058 | **E-mail** bookasia@hanmail.net
First published in Korea by Asia Publishers 2012
ISBN 978-89-94006-20-8(set) | 978-89-94006-22-2(04810)

K-픽션 시리즈 | Korean Fiction Series

〈K-픽션〉 시리즈는 한국문학의 젊은 상상력입니다. 최근 발표된 가장 우수하고 흥미로운 작품을 엄선하여 출간하는 〈K-픽션〉은 한국문학의 생생한 현장을 국내외 독자들과 실시간으로 공유하고자 기획되었습니다. 〈바이링궐 에디션 한국 대표 소설〉 시리즈를 통해 검증된 탁월한 번역진이 참여하여 원작의 재미와 품격을 최대한 살린 〈K-픽션〉 시리즈는 매 계절마다 새로운 작품을 선보입니다.

001 버핏과의 저녁 식사-**박민규** Dinner with Buffett-**Park Min-gyu**

002 아르판-**박형서** Arpan-**Park hyoung su**

003 애드벌룬-**손보미** Hot Air Balloon-**Son Bo-mi**

004 나의 클린트 이스트우드-**오한기** My Clint Eastwood-**Oh Han-ki**

005 이베리아의 전갈-**최민우** Dishonored-**Choi Min-woo**

006 양의 미래-**황정은** Kong's Garden-**Hwang Jung-eun**

007 대니-**윤이형** Danny-**Yun I-hyeong**

008 퇴근-**천명관** Homecoming-**Cheon Myeong-kwan**

009 옥화-**금희** Ok-hwa-**Geum Hee**

010 시차-**백수린** Time Difference-**Baik Sou linne**

011 올드 맨 리버-**이장욱** Old Man River-**Lee Jang-wook**

012 권순찬과 착한 사람들-**이기호** Kwon Sun-chan and Nice People-**Lee Ki-ho**

013 알바생 자르기-**장강명** Fired-**Chang Kang-myoung**

014 어디로 가고 싶으신가요-**김애란** Where Would You Like To Go?-**Kim Ae-ran**

015 세상에서 가장 비싼 소설-**김민정** The World's Most Expensive Novel-**Kim Min-jung**

016 체스의 모든 것-**김금희** Everything About Chess-**Kim Keum-hee**

017 할로윈-**정한아** Halloween-**Chung Han-ah**

018 그 여름-**최은영** The Summer-**Choi Eunyoung**

019 어느 피씨주의자의 종생기-**구병모** The Story of P.C.-**Gu Byeong-mo**

020 모르는 영역-**권여선** An Unknown Realm-**Kwon Yeo-sun**

021 4월의 눈-**손원평** April Snow-**Sohn Won-pyung**

022 서우-**강화길** Seo-u-**Kang Hwa-gil**

023 가출-**조남주** Run Away-**Cho Nam-joo**

024 연애의 감정학-**백영옥** How to Break Up Like a Winner-**Baek Young-ok**

025 창모-**우다영** Chang-mo-**Woo Da-young**

026 검은 방-**정지아** The Black Room-**Jeong Ji-a**

027 도쿄의 마야-**장류진** Maya in Tokyo-**Jang Ryu-jin**

028 홀리데이 홈-**편혜영** Holiday Home-**Pyun Hye-young**

029 해피 투게더-**서장원** Happy Together-**Seo Jang-won**

030 골드러시-**서수진** Gold Rush-**Seo Su-jin**

031 당신이 보고 싶어하는 세상-**장강명** The World You Want to See-**Chang Kang-myoung**

032 지난밤 내 꿈에-**정한아** Last Night, In My Dream-**Chung Han-ah**

Special 휴가중인 시체-**김중혁** Corpse on Vacation-**Kim Jung-hyuk**

Special 사파에서-**방현석** Love in Sa Pa-**Bang Hyeon-seok**

바이링궐 에디션 한국 대표 소설 목록

001 **병신과 머저리** 이청준 / 제니퍼 리

002 **어둠의 혼** 김원일 / 손석주, 캐서린 로즈 토레스

003 **순이삼촌** 현기영 / 이정희

004 **엄마의 말뚝 1** 박완서 / 유영난

005 **유형의 땅** 조정래 / 전경자

006 **무진기행** 김승옥 / 케빈 오록

007 **삼포 가는 길** 황석영/ 김우창

008 **아홉 켤레의 구두로 남은 사내** 윤흥길 / 브루스 풀턴, 주찬 풀턴

009 **돌아온 우리의 친구** 신상웅 / 손석주, 캐서린 로즈 토레스

010 **원미동 시인** 양귀자 / 전미세리

011 **중국인 거리** 오정희 / 주찬 풀턴, 브루스 풀턴

012 **풍금이 있던 자리** 신경숙 / 아그니타 테넌트

013 **하나코는 없다** 최윤 / 주찬 풀턴, 브루스 풀턴

014 **인간에 대한 예의** 공지영 / 주찬 풀턴, 브루스 풀턴

015 **빈처** 은희경 / 전승희

016 **필론의 돼지** 이문열 / 제이미 챙

017 **슬로우 불릿** 이대환 / 전승희

018 **직선과 독가스** 임철우 / 크리스 최

019 **깃발** 홍희담 / 전승희

020 **새벽 출정** 방현석 / 주다희, 안선재

021 **별을 사랑하는 마음으로** 윤후명 / 전미세리

022 **목련공원** 이승우 / 유진 라르센-할록

023 **칼에 찔린 자국** 김인숙 / 손석주, 캐서린 로즈 토레스

024 **회복하는 인간** 한강 / 전승희

025 **트렁크** 정이현 / 브루스 풀턴, 주찬 풀턴

026 **판문점** 이호철 / 테오도르 휴즈

027 **수난 이대** 하근찬 / 케빈 오록

055 **봄밤** 권여선 / 전승희

028 **분지** 남정현 / 전승희

029 **봄 실상사** 정도상 / 전승희

030 **은행나무 사랑** 김하기 / 손석주, 캐서린 로즈 토레스

031 **눈사람 속의 검은 항아리** 김소진 / 크리스 최

032 **오후, 가로지르다** 하성란 / 전승희

033 **나는 봉천동에 산다** 조경란 / 쉥크 카리

034 **그렇습니까? 기린입니다** 박민규 / 김소라

035 **성탄특선** 김애란 / 제이미 챙

036 **무자년의 가을 사흘** 서정인 / 제이미 챙

037 **유자소전** 이문구 / 제이미 챙

038 **향기로운 우물 이야기** 박범신 / 마야 웨스트

039 **월행** 송기원 / 제인 리

040 **협죽도 그늘 아래** 성석제 / 전승희

041 **아겔다마** 박상륭 / 전승희

042 **내 영혼의 우물** 최인석 / 전승희

043 **당신에 대해서** 이인성 / 마야 웨스트

044 **회색 시** 배수아 / 장정화, 앤드류 제임스 키스트

045 **브라운 부인** 정영문 / 정영문

046 **속옷** 김남일 / 전승희

047 **상하이에 두고 온 사람들** 공선옥 / 전승희

048 **모두에게 복된 새해** 김연수 / 마야 웨스트

049 **코끼리** 김재영 / 미셸 주은 김

050 **먼지별** 이경 / 전미세리

051 **혜자의 눈꽃** 천승세 / 전승희

052 **아베의 가족** 전상국 / 손석주

053 **문 앞에서** 이동화 / 전미세리

054 **그리고, 축제** 이혜경 / 브루스 풀턴, 주찬 풀턴

083 **상춘곡** 윤대녕 / 테레사 김

056 **오늘의 운세** 한창훈 / 케롱 린

057 **새** 전성태 / 전승희

058 **밀수록 다시 가까워지는** 이기호 / 테레사 김

059 **유리방패** 김중혁 / 케빈 오록

060 **전당포를 찾아서** 김종광 / 손석주

061 **도둑견습** 김주영 / 손석주

062 **사랑하라, 희망 없이** 윤영수 / 전승희

063 **봄날 오후, 과부 셋** 정지아 / 브랜든 맥케일, 김윤경

064 **유턴 지점에 보물지도를 묻다** 윤성희 / 이지은

065 **쁘이거나 쯔이거나** 백가흠 / 장정화, 앤드류 제임스 키스트

066 **나는 음식이다** 오수연 / 크리스 최

067 **트럭** 강영숙 / 전승희

068 **통조림 공장** 편혜영 / 미셸 주은 김

069 **꽃** 부희령 / 리처드 해리스, 김현경

070 **피의일요일** 윤이형 / 전승희

071 **북소리** 송영 / 손석주

072 **발칸의 장미를 내게 주었네** 정미경 / 스텔라 김

073 **아무도 돌아오지 않는 밤** 김숨 / 전미세리

074 **젓가락여자** 천운영 / 전미세리

075 **아직 일어나지 않은 일** 김미월 / 전미세리

076 **언니를 놓치다** 이경자 / 장정화, 앤드류 키스트

077 **아들** 윤정모 / 쉥크 카리

078 **명두** 구효서 / 미셸 주은 김

079 **모독** 조세희 / 손석주

080 **화요일의 강** 손홍규 / 제이미 챙

081 **고수** 이외수 / 손석주

082 **말을 찾아서** 이순원 / 미셸 주은 김

084 **삭매와 자미** 김별아 / 전미세리

085 **저만치 혼자서** 김훈 / 크리스 최

086 **감자** 김동인 / 케빈 오록

087 **운수 좋은 날** 현진건 / 케빈 오록

088 **탈출기** 최서해 / 박선영

089 **과도기** 한설야 / 전승희

090 **지하촌** 강경애 / 서지문

091 **날개** 이상 / 케빈 오록

092 **김 강사와 T 교수** 유진오 / 손석주

093 **소설가 구보씨의 일일** 박태원 / 박선영

094 **비 오는 길** 최명익 / 자넷 풀

095 **빛 속에** 김사량 / 크리스토퍼 스캇

096 **봄 · 봄** 김유정 / 전승희

097 **벙어리 삼룡이** 나도향 / 박선영

098 **달밤** 이태준 / 김종운, 브루스 풀턴

099 **사랑손님과 어머니** 주요섭 / 김종운, 브루스 풀턴

100 **갯마을** 오영수 / 마샬 필

101 **소망** 채만식 / 브루스 풀턴, 주찬 풀턴

102 **두 파산** 염상섭 / 손석주

103 **풀잎** 이효석 / 브루스 풀턴, 주찬 풀턴

104 **맥** 김남천 / 박선영

105 **꺼삐딴 리** 전광용 / 마샬 필

106 **소나기** 황순원 / 에드워드 포이트라스

107 **등신불** 김동리 / 설순봉

108 **요한 시집** 장용학 / 케빈 오록

109 **비 오는 날** 손창섭 / 전승희

110 **오발탄** 이범선 / 마샬 필

K-포엣 시리즈 | Korean Poet Series

030 앙코르-**신동옥** Encore-**Shin Dong-ok**

029 내가 가진 산책길을 다 줄게-**정우신**
I'll Give You All My Promenade-**Jeong Woo-shin**

028 글자만 남은 아침-**박장호** A Morning with only Writing Left-**Park Jang-ho**

027 거의 모든 기쁨-**이소연** Nearly All Happiness-**Lee Soyoun**

026 설운 일 덜 생각하고-**문동만** Thinking Less about Sad Things-**Moon Dong-man**

025 새를 따라서-**박철** Following Birds-**Park Cheol**

024 여기까지가 미래입니다-**황인찬**
You Have Reached the End of the Future-**Hwang Inchan**

023 비물질-**이현호** Non-matter-**Lee hyun-ho**

022 굴 소년들-**이설야** Cave Boys-**Lee Sul-ya**

021 끝을 시작하기-**김 근** Beginning the End-**Kim Keun**

020 호랑나비-**황규관** Tiger Swallowtail-**Hwang Gyu-gwan**

019 자살충-**김성규** Suicide Parasite-**Kim Seong-gyu**

018 호모 마스크스-**김수열** Homo Maskus-**Kim Soo-yeol**

017 해저의 교실에서 소년은 흰 달을 본다-**장이지**
A Boy Is Looking at the White Moon from a Classroom Under the Sea-**Jang I-**

016 느낌은 멈추지 않는다-**안주철** Feeling Never Stops-**Ahn Joo-cheol**

015 해피랜드-**김해자** HappyLand-**Kim Hae-ja**

014 마트료시카 시침핀 연구회-**유형진**
The Society for Studies in Matryoshka and Basting Pins-**Yu Hyoung-jin**

013 여름만 있는 계절에 네가 왔다-**이영주**
You Arrived in the Season of Perennial Summer-**Lee Young-ju**

012 세계의 끝에서 우리는-**양안다** We, At the End of the World-**Yang Anda**

011 깊은 일-**안현미** Deep Work-**An Hyeon-mi**

010 해를 오래 바라보았다-**이영광** I Gave the Sun a Long Look-**Lee Young-kwang**

009 유령시인-**김중일** A Ghost Poet-**Kim Joong-il**

008 자수견본집-**김정환** An Embroidery Sampler-**Kim Jung-whan**

007 저녁의 고래-**정일근** Evening of the Whale-**Chung Il-keun**

006 **김현 시선 Poems by Kim Hyun**

005 **안상학 시선 Poems by Ahn Sang-Hak**

004 **허수경 시선 Poems by Huh Sukyung**

003 **백석 시선 Poems by Baek Seok**

002 **안도현 시선 Poems by Ahn Do-Hyun**